PULLING FOCUS

MODEL LOVE

HJ WELCH

pulling Focus

hj welch

From this side of the lens, everything's fake. *Especially* the love.

MALYK

Listen, sweetie. I don't need anyone to protect me. But money is a problem right now and I desperately need this big break. So when my awful ex-boyfriend tries to take it all away from me, I'll do anything. Even pretend to be dating Mr. Hot Shot Photographer if it'll still get me through the door. I mean, he's offered to whisk me away to New York, and he's seriously gorgeous, so where's the problem? I can be professional. No one's going to catch feels.

OSCAR

I don't date models, especially not ones almost half my age. But beneath all of Malyk's bravado, I can see a sweet man who's hurting. It won't harm to pretend to be his boyfriend and spoil him during this ridiculous retreat to keep him safe, right? But there's something irresistible about him that's drawing me in, and suddenly a week doesn't seem long enough before he has to fly back to London. We're from different countries, different generations, different worlds entirely. It could never work. But when Malyk's ex threatens to cost him everything, I can't just stand back and let that happen, either.

Pulling Focus is a 60K word contemporary MM novel featuring an adventure across the Atlantic, a room with only one bed, bucket loads of explosive UST, a fabulous masquerade ball, and a long-suffering pooch who knows what his master needs better than he does. It's part of the *Model Love* multi-author series. Each book can be read as a standalone, in any order, but there are so many models falling in love, why not read them all?

Pulling Focus
Part of the Model Love multi author shared universe

Copyright © 2022 by HJ Welch

Cover design by Sleepy Fox Studio

For my dear friend, Susi.

I would have loved to work together again on this series like you hoped, but it wasn't meant to be. I'll never forget your kindness or your loving enthusiasm for happily ever afters and the authors who write them.

You are sorely missed, but you'll always be in our hearts.

Hx

1

————

MALYK

If this is actually going to be the end of my short-lived career as a model, I'd really rather I wasn't wearing a pair of fairy wings with my balls shoved up inside me with an industrial amount of gaffer tape.

You've got to laugh, don't you? How is this my life? Honestly. I wonder how drag queens manage to do this. I've needed to pee for half an hour, but there's no end in sight to the circus, so I need to be a good team player and just keep smiling.

We're on a full-day shoot. There's a dozen of us here getting ready, and it's chaos. Despite my discomfort, I'm also buzzing with excitement. This is what I love about my job. I get to help someone bring their vision to life. There's something quite lovely about being a part of a group working toward the same thing.

Not to mention I bloody love the attention. We've all got individual costumes, and my skin is all shimmery and shiny from the team of artists that fussed over me. I swish the scraps of fabric that float around my hips, and pretend I'm a wood nymph or something. I'm magical.

I'm *not* one step away from being kicked off the books for failing to get enough jobs. Today, I am successful. I am a star. I am going to work my arse off, and my luck will change.

I'm not going to let myself be humiliated by *certain people* no matter what.

I think the whole ethereal theme is supposed to come from some Shakespeare play. Like we're in a dream on the grounds of this fancy-schmancy manor house. But what we're dreaming of is androgyny and cheap-but-cheerful make-up.

"Don't be a brat. Don't be a brat," I whisper to myself as I wind my way past a row of girls—and I do mean girls. They can only be in their late teens—all sitting on the floor, helping each other tape up their boobs. We're all young and skinny here. You can practically smell the eating disorders.

Ew.

I feel sorry for the models I meet who chew some gum and call that dinner. Not me. I'm sure my metabolism will catch up with me eventually, but until then, I'll eat whatever the hell I like and burn off the excess at the gym or in someone else's bed.

Actually, I'm kind of looking forward to gaining a few inches (nooo—not *those* kinds of inches, although I'll never say no). Being too skinny has cost me so much work. Not masculine enough for most commercial modeling, so it seems. I'd be perfect for runways just as I am, but, well…

I need a better back catalog portfolio. Or to meet the right person. It's all about connections in this industry. Until then, I'm apparently not only too skinny but also too fem, too Black (or not Black enough—go figure), too mouthy, just…too much.

Always too much.

But not today. Today I am going to go home with a wad of cash money, and that's why I keep smiling as I make my way out of the house toward the area I've been told to wait, hanging on the arrival of whoever this photographer is who we're all supposed to be quivering and panting for. I heard he's *way* too posh for some high-street cosmetics brand, normally. But when the other guy had to bail for personal reasons, it seems that this bloke came to save the day as a personal favor to Mr. McKay.

That's right. The actual Marcus McKay himself. I've only met the owner of our agency once, but he's a scrummy silver fox. Hopefully, his friend will be just as hot. Bonus points if he knows which way to point a lens.

Because despite the massive discomfort I'm in between my legs and how ridiculous I feel in this floaty get-up, I have to admit the make-up department and costumers know their stuff. I look absolutely lush. Maybe this will be a shoot I can be proud of for once.

It's already my favorite from the last few months for the amount it's paying. My god, I'll actually be able to afford rent next week without having to starve myself. Remember? Already skinny enough. Ohhh, perhaps I'll pick up some fish and chips for dinner on the way home. Maybe a bottle of that half-decent cheap white wine I discovered. Yes, if I can make it through the next few hours, I'm celebrating.

Lord knows I'll have earned it.

I've been trying to ignore Chris Oakley all afternoon. It's rare agents come to shoots, but I guess this one's a big deal for McKay's as it's all our talent. It galls me that Chris was the one to swing the deal, because everyone's been singing his praises for weeks now. This brand might be a high-street one, but it's still a household name and turns a hell of a profit. It's big news that they've made this new advertising campaign so explicitly queer, and even bigger news that McKay's models are exclusively the faces of that campaign.

I guess it makes sense that they'd choose us. Mr. McKay is gay himself. He used to be a model, but he left his agency when they tried to keep him closeted. I love that he retaliated by setting up his own agency, whose mission statement is to be as inclusive as possible. So yes, it made sense that the brand picked us to work with. But the fact that it's our agency only is a pretty big coup. Everyone involved should feel honored.

If anything, the fact that Chris was in charge of casting should make me feel even luckier to be here.

Oh, yeah. Another reason I struggle to get work?

I used to shag my own agent like a complete amateur.

I walked in on him fucking some random dude and refused to suck his cock since. Obviously, I can't *prove* that's why my work dried up, but I'm sure it isn't helping. And I haven't found a way to request another agent without explaining why. *I'm* the one who'll get treated like an untrustworthy ho if I spill, I'm sure, so I've kept my gob shut.

It takes everything to play nice when I see him. Especially when I walk up to the area where we're going to be shooting, and catch him leaning in close to a newbie who I know for a fact is barely seventeen.

The boy is looking up at Chris with wide eyes, like that idiot is bestowing pearls of wisdom upon him.

Nope. Not having that.

"Oh, no. You've come undone, gorgeous," I say in a playful tone as I step up behind the innocent little sweetie. With a tug of just one finger, I manage to unravel the bow at the top of his corset. That way, when Chris glances over, I'm not making a liar out of myself. "Let me help you with that! We want you *perrrfect*, don't we?"

"Y-yes," the boy says, his voice trembling almost as much as his slender body.

I fake a brilliant smile at my ex like there's nothing wrong in the world. "Heya, Chris," I say and scrunch up my nose a little. "I think one of the girls said she had Mr. McKay on the phone for you. Said it was urgent."

He snatches his own mobile out of his pocket, probably looking for a missed call. He hasn't got one because of course Mr. McKay isn't calling him from New York. But I know that stroking his ego is the only way to get him to bugger off.

"Shit. Okay, thanks."

He runs off like he doesn't know me from Adam. Just some model passing on a message. Whatever. I don't want him to treat me like I'm special anymore. That's what gets you in trouble.

I dip my head down to whisper in the young lad's ear. "Never be alone in a room with him," I say, my tone completely serious now.

The boy blinks at me as I withdraw. But I just smile and rub his arm, having retied the bow on his back. I hope he understands. There are people listening in, and I don't want to be accused of spreading malicious gossip.

Even if it is true.

"Don't you look stunning?" I say genuinely with a warm smile. "This your first shoot?"

"Th-third," he stammers. "It's the fanciest one. Usually, it's just a white backdrop in some warehouse. Hey, um, you're Malyk Defries, right? I love your Insta. I probably like all your posts like a loser." He giggles nervously.

He's being sweet, so I sigh internally rather than out loud. People often just read my name and don't hear it, so they tend to pronounce it *Mal*-ec rather than Mal-*eek*. I'm super proud of how I've built up my socials, though. It's what got me signed in the first place. So I don't correct him like a dick. Hopefully, he'll realize his mistake down the line.

"Aww, thanks," I say with a wink. "What's your handle? I'll follow you back."

His jaw drops. "S-seriously? That would be amazing. Um…"

He rattles off a name that I commit to memory. My phone's tucked away in my bag, but I promise him I'll remember. I've had a lot of practice doing that. I don't like to have my phone ruining my outfit at parties, but I definitely like to message the hotties afterward.

Not that I'll be hitting on this boy. He's got enough creeps thirsting after him, I'm sure.

"Good afternoon, everyone," a light, amused voice like honey drifts over the chatter. The American accent immediately gets my attention, and I whip my head around.

Welp. I guess this is the photographer everyone's been so rabid about. My mouth goes dry, and my heart feels like it's either going to slam out of my chest or flatline. Nothing in between.

This wasn't part of the plan.

I'm not even sure why I've got cartoon love hearts spinning around my head all of a sudden. In my line of work, I'm surrounded by godlike men all the time. Strong jaws, smooth, hard abs, perfect teeth—everything this industry sells to the public as being the dream. But this guy…

Well, he's older. In his late thirties or early forties, I'd guess. He's kind of scruffy with a golden beard that could probably do with a trim. Over his hair, he's wearing a baseball cap that looks decades old. His jeans definitely aren't designer, and his plaid shirt is half tucked in, half hanging out.

But as his gaze sweeps over the waiting models, he sort of…well…*sparkles*. Like he's just walked into a jewelry store, and he's not only delighted by the wears, but the diamonds are reflecting off his bright, hazel eyes.

His thighs are straining against the denim wrapped around them, and his shoulders are broad and strong. But—you know what? Out of all those things, I think it might be the way that his blunt fingers caress the camera in his grasp like it's a familiar lover that's really set my heart racing. That's probably ridiculous. Lord, I've snorted too much fairy dust. I just can't take my eyes off his hands, though, as they carefully handle the protruding lens. There's power in that grip, but also a tenderness.

Aaaannnnd *breathe*, Malyk! I'm so wound up about Chris that I'm lusting after the first man that walks my way?

Well…that's not really true. I haven't had this kind of reaction to a guy in a very long time.

And I can't have it now. This job has to go well. So I stand tall and try and look interested, but not *too* interested, among the gaggle of models that have congregated by the fountain. Except…did I imagine it? Or did Mr. Photographer's sparkling eyes linger just a little longer on me?

I try not to preen, but I roll my shoulders back and relax with a small smile. If I catch his attention, that means a higher chance of being more prominently featured in the shoot. This could still be my lucky day after all.

"My apologies, Mr. Wainwright," Chris says as he strides up to the photographer, buttoning up his jacket and smoothing back his hair. "I had to make a phone call. Is everything arranged to an acceptable standard?"

What he's really asking is, are us models up to scratch. I brace myself in case we start getting cut on the spot. That would mean we'd get paid travel expenses, and maybe an hour or two's rate, but not for the full day.

But Mr. Wainwright just beams, looking around at the foliage around us, the impressive fountain, and then at our group standing anxiously in front of him. "No, everything's wonderful. And it's Oscar, please."

Chris grins. He loves making friends with important people. I personally get it from a networking perspective, but he's the kind that likes to climb the ladder, then pull it up behind him so no one else can get the same chance or possibly take an opportunity away from him.

Urgh, how did I ever fancy him? I know he's got a rocking bod and epic cock, but I really should have seen what a wanker he was long before I caught him cheating.

Mr. Wainwright—I mean Oscar—starts directing us to various positions around the fountain, and draping us against ornamental bird baths and the surrounding trees. When he comes to instruct me, I get a thrill when he places his hands on me to get the pose just right. His skin is warm, and although his focus is on my limbs, and not my face, I can see that sparkle up close and personal.

"Thank you," I murmur when he finishes. His gaze flicks up and locks with mine, causing a ripple of desire over my body. *Bollocks.* Hopefully, I don't look like a pining teenager with a hopeless crush.

"You're very welcome," he says back.

God, he's so *calm.* It's like an anchor in a turbulent sea. I forget about my ex and my rent, and just keep my mind on doing a good job for him. That's suddenly become very important to me.

It's also not escaped my attention that he's seated me right at the front of the fountain. That doesn't mean anything necessarily, but it's better than being hidden away at the back. He also pairs the sweet newbie—Jamie—with me, so I get the added bonus of making sure he's okay with Chris still flitting around.

Speaking of which, my douchebag ex is hovering like a fruit fly as Oscar starts to get to work. I try to ignore his inane chatter about industry events. He's obviously trying to impress the hotshot American with all the people he knows. I'm surprised that Oscar doesn't seem too bothered by Chris, even though he must be distracting the photographer while he's trying to work.

But then my stomach drops.

"So, I'll be seeing you at Honeyrock next week, right?" Chris asks, trying to sound casual. "I figured because that's your stomping ground. And obviously the best of the best will be there."

That's next week already?

Honeyrock is an annual retreat hosted by one of New York's most successful but also eccentric designers, Emmalina, in one of her country mansions. It's strictly invitation-only to a week-long event that sounds like something out of a bohemian dream. Decadent pool parties, impromptu mini-catwalks, and photo shoots with next season's wears. But the networking—*urgh, lord!* The networking is what it's all about. Honeyrock has launched so many careers within the Haus of Emmalina. It's a once-in-a-lifetime opportunity.

And I've got a ticket.

Or…at least I *had* a ticket.

Fuck, shit, bollocks! Chris asked me months ago. If I'm being brutally honest, I think I knew at the time that he got off on being able to offer me this incredible thing. He liked the power it held over me. But I didn't care, I just cried my eyes out and thanked the universe for such a lucky break.

It's never occurred to me since the breakup what that would mean for Honeyrock.

"I'll be there," says Oscar casually. He's focusing on a couple of girls covered in flowers and butterflies who are pressed up on either side of a sturdy tree trunk. "That's it. Really beautiful," he murmurs, getting them to look a couple of different ways before having a word with the lighting guy to make some adjustments.

Up until now, I was trying to soak up every line of direction he's been giving to the models to try and apply everything he's saying when it comes to my time in front of the lens. But now my heart is in my mouth. I'm going to have to talk to Chris after all and ask what's happening. He was going to pay for my flights and everything. I can't lose this opportunity. I just can't.

Except, I'm not sure if I even really had it in the first place. Did he ever intend to take me? Or was that just another way he tried to dazzle and control me?

I get my answer after his next breath.

"I'll be flying solo, so it would be cool to maybe meet up while we're both in the city. We can discuss the campaign." He waves his hand around to encompass the shoot.

I don't think he even sees me.

Apparently, that doesn't stop my giant gob from firing off.

"What the *fuck?*" I cry out in horror before I even realize what I've done.

Oh lord. Everyone's head jerks in my direction, and I do mean everyone. My fellow models, the technicians, make-up and hair artists, other agents, but especially Chris and Oscar. Strangely, what makes my cheeks flame with shame the most isn't my ex-boyfriend's eyes widening with incredulity. It's the look of confusion on Oscar's face. Like I care what some (really hot) guy I just met thinks.

"Malyk?" the newbie Jamie whispers next to me.

Chris's face has rearranged itself into cool anger. "Is there a problem, Defries?"

Fucking 'Defries.' Is he kidding me?

Well, my foot is already in it. I might as well jump all the way in.

"You told me I was going with you," I say firmly, trying to keep my heart from exploding out of my chest. "You said I had a ticket and that you'd booked the flights." He'd *promised* me, the bastard. But I never saw any proof. No receipts. It's dawning on me that I've been a completely gullible moron, but that doesn't stop the tears from pooling in my eyes or my voice from getting choked up.

He knows perfectly well what he'd be taking away from me. That's obvious when he laughs in my face.

"Are you joking?" he scoffs. "Why would I invite someone nobody knows? It's this kind of attitude that keeps getting you in trouble, Defries. Now are you going to behave, or do I need to remove you from the set?"

The humiliation is unreal. Not only has he dashed my dreams on the rocks, but he's also patronizing me in front of dozens of people. My mouth opens and closes a couple of times as my eyes burn, but I manage to blink away the tears and wrestle back some composure.

"S-sorry," I whisper. "I…I must have gotten confused."

He smirks at me. Jamie squeezes my hand. I'm tempted to snatch it away, but there's a part of me that recognizes he's being kind. I feel vulnerable, and I hate that, but I'm also not in a position to throw away a friend right now. So I squeeze his fingers back, honestly grateful not to be completely alone in such a terrible moment.

People slowly look away from the scene I just created, focusing again on their own work.

All except Oscar.

He's got a strange look on his face as he studies me. Great. Now he thinks I'm a freak as well, I bet.

So much for this being my lucky day. I'm not sure if Chris will even keep me on McKay's books after that little outburst I had. Hopefully, I'll still get paid for today, but I certainly don't feel like celebrating anymore.

Earlier, it seemed like my career might just be taking flight.

Now my wings have been clipped.

Is this the end?

2

OSCAR

I'm definitely missing something here.

I was already feeling a little irked because this gentleman was doing his darndest to interfere with my process, but now he's upset one of my models.

One of my really enchantingly beautiful models.

The young man looks mortified, trembling on the edge of the fountain and obviously trying not to lose it. He's barely dressed in scraps of earthy-colored materials with golden leaves stuck to his shimmering light brown skin. His dark hair is shaved close at the sides with a gradual fade up, and the top is a mop of tight curls with gold glitter sprinkled in.

He looks exposed. Vulnerable.

It's those piercing eyes that are breaking my heart, though. When I arrived, they were shining with enthusiasm and hope. I already knew he was going to be stunning on film. But now they're brimming with unshed tears.

Professionally, I'm annoyed at this Oakley guy for

messing with my subjects. It's people like him who are making me seriously think of quitting the fashion industry altogether and switching to nature and wildlife. There's so much ego and bullshit. You don't get that from birds or trees.

Personally, there's something that feels like a caveman trying to claw its way out of me to protect this delicate soul and make everything okay.

Usually, I'm pretty Zen. I've been there, done that. I learned a long time ago there's no sense in getting all riled up about something when most of the time it's just going to blow over one way or another anyhow. But the sense of powerlessness rolling off this young man is rubbing me all the wrong ways. It's not helped when the guy who's supposed to be in charge of this whole shoot laughs at him.

Quietly, something inside me snaps. Like a twig deep in a forest. It doesn't matter if no one else is around to hear, the sound still cracks through the air, and the world has now subtly changed.

"Well, that's pretty lucky you don't have a spare ticket after all, Chris," I say, shaking my head like this is all mildly amusing instead of the mad plan that's forming in my brain as the words come spilling out of my mouth. I whistle and wink at the young man before grinning at Oakley. "That would have gotten awkward pretty fast."

"Awkward?" he repeats with a frown, but my attention is already back on the young man. Defries, Oakley called him. He's truly stunning. I've seen a hell of a lot of people over the years in this industry, and I have a knack for spying who has real potential.

This guy could go stratospheric under the right circumstances.

That's ultimately what keeps me talking. I feel an unreasonable urge to stick it to this jerk who thought it necessary to humiliate a vulnerable young person in front of his peers. But I also sense I'm looking at someone with a dazzling career on the horizon. Selfishly, I want to snap him up before anyone else does. I want to be the one to open the door and hold his hand as he walks through.

It's been so long since I felt this way about a model. I've had experiences with muses before, and I fully appreciate the concept, but this charming soul is making me itch with ideas in a way I haven't felt for years.

Plus, I'd be a heartless bastard not to see what kind of an opportunity he was mourning right in front of my eyes.

"Awkward, how?" Oakley demands, suspicion already creeping into his voice. *Boy, is he going to be in for a shock,* I think gleefully to myself.

Outwardly, I shrug. "Unfortunately, you've ruined my surprise. But, babe" —I smile at the young man— "you *do* have an invitation to Honeyrock. I was going to tell you over dinner tonight."

There's a beat where everyone's looking at me. I hope no one ruins my little charade, most of all the young man I'm still smiling at. Our eyes are locked. When I was adjusting his position earlier, I noticed they were a beautiful greenish gray. Unusual for his skin tone.

Now, they go wide, and I can practically see his thoughts whirling. I give him time, hoping he catches on to my little game.

"Malyk," the boy next to him hisses. "Are you *dating* Oscar Wainwright?"

"Uhhh…" he says, his eyes flicking anxiously over to Oakley.

Ah. Yes, that makes sense. I'd bet a million bucks they were dating—or at least fucking—and this smooth talker promised my new little muse, Malyk, the world. And now he's taken it all away because he can.

"Of course they're not," Oakley scoffs with a particularly unkind laugh.

I turn and hold his gaze until he stops smirking. "We met last week, actually. He's exactly the kind of fresh face Emmalina is looking for. It was my pleasure to procure him an invitation."

Or rather that I have a standard plus-one invite every year that I never use. Linny's going to be absolutely thrilled if I turn up with this young man. Even if it's just as friends.

"That way," I continue, "we could keep seeing each other, and he could experience a truly spectacular opportunity." I look back and give Malyk an apologetic smile. "Not how I wanted to break the news, but I hope you're happy, sweetheart."

He's staring at me with his jaw hanging open. The cute kid next to him is bouncing on the spot, shaking Malyk's hand clasped between his own. "*Oh my god,*

Malyk!" he whispers a little too loudly, but Malyk is still just fixated on me.

It appears Oakley has recovered. "If you were dating, you'd know it's pronounced Mal-*eek* not *Mal-ec*," he says smugly.

"It is?" the cute kid asks in horror.

I hum briefly. I was careful not to use his name because I wasn't sure what he prefers to be called, and I'm glad that's paid off. "I wasn't going to embarrass a new model in front of an audience," I say pointedly to Oakley.

He gets I'm not just talking about the kid.

"Oscar, thank you," Malyk finally splutters. He rises and walks over to me barefoot, clutching his hands to his chest. He's willowy, but there's a power in his limbs that makes me appreciate him even more.

Professionally, of course. My admiration is strictly from an aesthetic point of view. Like an artist appreciating a beautiful landscape.

It would be wildly inappropriate for me to have any kind of reaction as he gently touches my shoulders and presses a kiss to my cheek. So I don't feel a warmth rushing through me. I certainly don't feel my pants tightening. Nope. We're all good here.

"I don't know what to say," the young man says breathlessly as he shakes his head.

He's got an accent I can't quite place, but it's like music to my ears. What he's really asking is if I'm fucking with him, I'm sure. His light eyes dance as they search my face, so I reach up and squeeze his arm where it won't smudge any make-up.

"We can discuss it all over dinner," I tell him just loud enough so Oakley can hear. "You're still good to come with me after we've finished work, yeah?"

"Y-yes," he says with a nod, like that had been our secret little plan all along. Like we've been enjoying a romantic interlude these past several days without anyone knowing, and the cat's finally out of the bag.

His face splits into a stunning smile, and his expression is filled with genuine affection and appreciation. He's not a greedy little brat, I can tell. The apprehension I was feeling embarking on such a harebrained scheme is diminishing by the minute.

There are tears in his pretty eyes again, but not the same distraught ones as before. "This certainly is a big surprise," he says, his voice all fluttery.

For us both, I think in amusement.

"Alright, sweetheart. We should probably get back to work. Sorry, Chris, for the disruption," I add.

I smile at the other man in the way I've practiced over my many years in this industry because so much of it is completely fake. I don't mean one word of my apology, but I make him think I do. I make him think it *was* me and Malyk who caused the shoot to pause, and not him and his gloating nastiness. There's a calmness in that fakeness.

And then I look at Malyk, knowing that's all fake too. But as I rub his arm and send him to sit back down, it doesn't feel inauthentic in the slightest.

I'm not sure what I've gotten myself into here, but I *do* know that I'm going to take that sweet, sassy man out to a ridiculously fancy restaurant tonight. And if possible, I'm going to convince him to fly out to America with a total stranger. First class, of course, with lounge access. All the perks that never normally bother me but suddenly feel quite important if I get to share them with Malyk Defries.

Something tells me he's not had many nice things in this life.

There's no real danger here, anyway. I have a policy to never get involved with models, that I've never even come close to breaking throughout my career. It just seems like a recipe for disaster, not to mention an abuse of power. Looking at Oakley and what he's just done to Malyk in front of my eyes, I'm even more convinced of my resolve.

No, Malyk will be safe with me because I'll *keep* him safe.

So I might be strict in my no-feelings rule. *Definitely* in my hands-off rule. But there's no reason I can't spoil the man just a little with a once-in-a-lifetime trip.

I think it would make us both happy.

3

MALYK

"I'm really sorry I pronounced your name wrong," Jamie frets sweetly by my side.

I nudge my shoulder against his. "A lot of people do if they just read it online," I assure him. "Thank you for holding my hand just then."

The shoot has quietened down again, especially since Chris huffed and said something about needing to make some calls before marching off. Just so long as we all knew how busy and important he is before he left in a sulk, I guess that's all that matters to him.

I try to repress a grin. No matter what happens, it feels *really good* to have had someone on my side showing that prick up.

My gaze follows Oscar as he works. He's with a different guy now, one of the ones on the bird feeders. He's wearing a flowery toga that's draped elegantly over one shoulder, but it's offset ever-so-coolly with a jaunty black top hat on his head. Oscar is talking to him like he talks to everyone as he works with them. Like they matter. Like they're the only person in the whole world.

That's why I'm trying not to read too much into that nonsense he spouted off, because it was nonsense. It took me ages to work out that he was trying to pretend we'd been seeing each other or something. However, I'm incredibly grateful for it. Even if I only get the chance to say a heartfelt thank-you once we've finished the shoot, that will be fine. He completely saved my day.

Well, not completely. I'm still mourning the loss of my spectacular big break. I'm trying to console myself that I almost certainly never had that opportunity to begin with, but right now, that feels like cold comfort. In time, I'm hoping it will fade, and I'll be able to see the truth.

You can't lose what you never had.

In this moment, I just keep reminding myself what kindness a stranger has done me. He helped me save face when Chris was trying his hardest to crush me down.

Urgh! The nerve of some men! He's acting like *I* cheated on *him*. The gall. Well, I guess that's the way this world works. Those with power keep it by stepping on anyone beneath them.

"Are you *really* dating Mr. Wainwright?" Jamie asks in awe.

Seeing as we're not being photographed or seen to by any of the make-up people, it's okay to have a little chitchat. I don't want to lie to the lad, though, so I just tap my nose and wink.

"She'd never kiss and tell, love," I say conspiratorially. "She's a lady."

Jamie giggles and his eyes light up, probably convinced that I'm sitting on a delicious secret. That's okay. It's just a little white lie to save face. After all, I *do* feel like Oscar and I have shared something intimate just now, even if it was a little bizarre.

Hark at me! 'Oscar.' I really need to keep thinking of him as Mr. Wainwright, but try as I might, I just can't.

I think it's that warm smile. He doesn't look like a 'Mr.' That's something you call a teacher or the bloke at the bank. He feels like a mate.

A seriously hot, older, super rich and super successful mate. The kind you went to school with and could be envious of how well he's made it, but instead, you're just happy for him because he's a decent bloke, too. There's something that feels like he deserved it.

Bloody hell, there I go again, romanticizing this near stranger because he did one kind thing for me. This is how I end up in trouble. All those abandonment daddy issues leading me right into the arms of manipulative arseholes, yuck. He clearly saw what Chris had done and just has crazy intuition, so he was able to come up with a clever story. It's impressive, but it's not a marriage proposal.

I need to get a grip.

The remainder of the shoot goes by in a bit of a blur. Oscar gets a couple of dozen shots with me and Jamie, then he takes me by myself to get some more woodsy snaps. I try not to read too much into that. I try not to feel special. It's just a job. He's just trying to do what's best for the brand.

But I can't deny that if I can be a part of what's best for the brand…well, that's the whole reason I love being a model. I want to help bring people's visions to life.

For the rest of the afternoon, I daydream about possibly being one of the faces of this LGBT plus campaign, and it fills me with hope and joy. It might not be Honeyrock, but it's not nothing, which is what Chris obviously wanted to leave me with earlier.

Finally, mercifully, we're allowed to leave, and I full on *run* to the nearest bathroom. I carefully untuck and manage to have that wee I needed a couple of hours ago. Then I head back up to where I left all my things, not caring if my junk is visible in my underwear now.

I'm done being a nymph. Time to get back to the real world.

I groan as I carefully peel off my ensemble, handing it back to one of the wardrobe people, and flex my aching muscles. Jeans and a T-shirt feel heavenly after all that.

I'm done with the make-up with just a quick scrub with a baby wipe. Then I just splash my skin with a little water and rub in some of the cheap moisturizer I keep in my bag for after the gym. I'll make sure to do my proper routine when I get home.

Right now, I have to find Oscar.

He mentioned something vague about me meeting him back down by the fountain, but I don't really expect him to be there. I'd have thought he'd be mixing with the agents or have left entirely. Except…there he is.

When I run back outside, he's all alone, perched on the fountain—the same spot I'd spent most of the afternoon.

I tell myself it doesn't mean anything. Because it doesn't. So what? That was probably just the most convenient place to wait. Or maybe it has the best light to be studying the back of his camera like he's doing. I imagine he's going over his work, and I feel a sudden flutter in my belly.

I wonder how my photos turned out.

"Ah, Malyk," he says brightly in that gooey American accent of his. Chris said he was from New York, and it sounds like an East Coast lilt to my uncultured ear. It's certainly not a heavy Bronx twang or anything. I'm mostly ridiculously impressed that he pronounced my name right. He beckons me. "I was just admiring your work."

I do as he asks and edge closer, suddenly nervous. Look, I know I'm a stunner, all right? It would be kind of a dick move to pretend like I don't know I was blessed with good genes. But that's not *work*. Work is what he does with the lenses and the focus and the framing. It's what all the make-up and costume and lighting people do. I'm just the lucky bitch that gets to be in the spotlight.

But as I look down at the image Oscar is offering up to me, I have to admit I do it *good.*

I gasp and touch my chest, genuinely taken aback by how stunning I am. It's one of the shots of just me sprawled out against the fountain, and the light is hitting me *just* right so I seem…ethereal. Like I actually could be from an enchanted forest.

I'm not even thinking about cosmetics in that moment. If that's the only photograph I have to represent my entire time on this planet, I think I'd be happy. I mean, it's not going to stop me from taking a million billion selfies for the rest of my life, but if I end up in the history books, that's the image I want beside my name.

"Thank you," I whisper, embarrassed by how my voice catches. I paw at my throat and laugh, trying to cover it up. He doesn't need to see me get all mushy. I want him to respect me. "Bugger me!" I cry loudly. "That's a cracking one. I'm going to use that for my Christmas cards this year."

Like I have anyone to send Chrissy cards to, but he doesn't need to know how pathetic I am.

He hums, and I'm not sure what he's thinking. But then he sighs happily and turns the screen off, looking up at me with a smile that makes my heart flip. "So… about that dinner," he says casually.

I feel my eyebrows rise up, and I'm about to blow a raspberry and wave my hand dismissively. But what he did for me today should probably have been accompanied by a white horse, it was so damned noble.

"That was so unspeakably kind how you saved me today," I say quietly, my gaze dropping to the ground. "Thank you. But you don't need to pretend anymore. There's no one here to tattle to Chris."

It's unprofessional, but I can't stop myself from rolling my eyes as his name falls out of my mouth.

What a twat. Still, he's an acquaintance of Oscar's, so I need to behave. But when I look back at him, he's just watching me with a curious expression.

"I thought we should go to dinner to discuss the details," he says earnestly. "But if you're uncomfortable with that, I'll happily email you everything and make sure you're fully prepared."

Despite my absolute best efforts, my heart is thumping in my chest. What's he on about now?

I lick my lips and glance down at his camera before looking him in the eye again. "You mean the photos? I'd appreciate a copy of that one for sure, but the rest you can just send to the office like normal. I assume you've worked with McKay's before?" I hope that doesn't come across as condescending or anything. I'm sure the man knows how to do his job. But I'm at a loss as to what he can mean.

He raises an eyebrow. It shouldn't be as sexy as it is. There's still the whole baseball cap and scruffy beard situation that I know I mentioned before. But fuck my life, it's making my cock more tingly than the damn gaffer tape.

"You're not interested in going to Honeyrock?" he asks.

Whoosh. That's all the air rushing out of my lungs.

"H-Honeyrock?" I stutter. "Of course I'm bloody interested, but you were just being nice."

Oscar gets to his feet. He has a calm, unthreatening presence. He's a fraction shorter than me and pretty solid. I can appreciate this now we're standing face-to-face.

"Was I?" he replies to my statement about him just being nice. Then he crooks his sodding arm like an actual gentleman. "I assume Italian food is okay. Or we could go Thai."

For a second, I don't move.

Then I realize how monumentally stupid it would be to pass up this offer purely because I'm confused. So I shake myself and laugh, slipping my arm through his. "Thai, please. I like it a little spicy."

And if that ain't god's honest truth.

4

OSCAR

Malyk is looking around the restaurant in quiet awe. He doesn't strike me as someone who's usually lost for something to say. I try not to study him while he's distracted, but it's hard. He's got such a captivating face and a liquid way to his movements.

He rests his chin on the back of his long fingers, his gray-green eyes roaming the darkened restaurant. It's decorated with artificial trees all around the walls, their branches reaching over the ceiling entwined with fairy lights. One of the partitions has a small waterfall running down it into a pond filled with colorful fish. A golden Buddha watches over the patrons as they eat, and there's gentle wind chime type music floating through the air. It could come across as hokey, but instead, it feels like we stepped from the busy city street into an Asian paradise.

"Have you decided what you'd like yet?" I ask, bringing Malyk's attention back to me. Or more specifically, to me and then the menu that's open in front of him. I didn't miss the way his eyes went wide as soon as he opened it. He said he liked Thai food, so I don't think he's intimidated by an unfamiliar selection.

No. He's seen the prices.

Money is such a strange concept to me. Don't get me wrong, I vividly remember being poor in my youth. I just think everyone should have access to everything. Once I got to a point where I didn't have to worry about my bank balance anymore, it gave me great peace to just not have to think about it. I honestly couldn't tell you what's in any of my accounts right now except that it's 'enough,' and I know that makes me a lucky son of a gun.

I get enormous pleasure giving other people that feeling as well, even sweet young men I've only just met. Although I can't say I flash my cash around to *meet* young men. That would be extremely strange.

Anyway, the point I'm trying to make is that Malyk doesn't seem to realize tonight's on me, and he's worrying, which isn't necessary. In fact, after the day he's had, that's the last thing I want. So I smile warmly like nothing's amiss.

"It all looks so good, doesn't it? Why don't we get one of the set menus for two? This selection looks tasty." I reach over and tap the one I mean on his menu so he can take a look. "Remember, this is my treat," I say casually, hoping he takes my meaning.

He doesn't have to spend a dime. Or a penny, I guess, seeing as we're in London.

He takes a breath and laces his fingers together. "Why are you being so nice to me?"

It's blunt. I like blunt.

"Because that agent of yours treated you appallingly today," I say equally plainly. "He promised you an opportunity of a lifetime, then laughed at you in front of a crowd when he snatched it away." I shrug. "Such a negative act deserved an equally positive act to balance the universe out."

He shakes his head. "But you're not *really* offering to take me to Honeyrock, are you?"

"I am," I say simply. "I've got a plus-one that's going to waste. Why shouldn't it go to you?"

"Because I haven't earned it," he splutters, as if that's obvious.

I raise my eyebrows. "Yet you earned an invitation when it came from Oakley?"

It's his turn to shrug and glance his eyes away. "We were dating. Or fucking, at least. I thought he was being nice. Maybe." His gaze snaps back up, suddenly steely. "Are you expecting me to fuck you?"

I choke on my own spit and have to bang my chest a couple of times. "Um, no," I say when I'm recovered, then sip some of the table water. "No, absolutely not."

His mouth twitches. "You calling me a minger?"

I can tell he's teasing, probably to cover his own insecurities. I'm pretty sure that's British slang for someone unfortunate looking. I arch a disapproving eyebrow at him.

"No, I'm not," I say patiently. "You're an extremely attractive young man."

His mouth twitches again, this time in pleasure. It shouldn't matter, but I like that he likes that I think he's hot. Well, anyone with eyes could tell him that, couldn't they? I temper down the thrill that bubbles through me.

He's right to suspect a form of 'payment,' especially if his previous invitation came from someone he was involved with. But I need to make it crystal clear that never even crossed my mind because it didn't.

No matter how pretty his plump lips are or how many times I've caught myself wondering what it might be like to kiss them. That is strictly off-limits.

"This is a business prospect—for both of us," I elaborate. "You look amazing on camera, and I know how to wield one, so it seems like a good opportunity for us both to get to show our skills."

"All right, we've established I'm a snack," he says, pulling his fingers gently through each other. I have to drag my gaze away from them. "But forgive me if I'm still suspicious. *Nothing* comes for free in this life."

"You're right," I agree. "You'd still have to work hard and impress the right people if you want to get anywhere with Emmalina. I'm not giving you anything. I'm just helping you get through the door."

He licks his lips. "And that's really it? No hidden strings?"

I shake my head. "I like giving back. You seem like you'd flourish if you just got the chance. Like today."

His eyes light up. "Did you really like my work earlier?" he asks. It's not coming from a place of conceit, I don't think. He's genuinely eager to know if he did a good job for me.

That right there is why I know I've made the right decision.

"There was a lot of talent today," I say diplomatically. "But what you gave to the camera was astonishing. I think you'll be featuring prominently in the final campaign."

He bites his lower lip and grins, looking down for a second as he absorbs the compliment. "Thank you," he says softly, just like he did when I showed him my favorite shot of him by the fountain.

"You're welcome," I assure him. "I see real potential in you, Malyk. I honestly think Emmalina will want to meet you. I wouldn't offer you this invitation if I didn't believe that you could truly make the most of it. I don't back lame horses."

He holds my gaze like he's weighing my words very carefully. The air between us starts to feel charged. I don't react other than to maintain the gaze, letting him know he can trust me.

"If you, with all your experience and skill, think I have a real shot..." he says eventually with a tilt of his head, "then that means I *have* earned it." He thrusts his hand out over the table toward me. "I accept your invitation and promise not to let you down, Mr. Wainwright."

I grin and take his hand, shaking it once firmly. "The only person you have to promise not to let down is yourself. That's all I ask."

"Okay, then," he says quietly. His eyes are positively ablaze as I let his fingers trail through mine, and we separate.

It's okay. He can flirt. Now that I've assured him that I don't expect any kind of sexual favors, he can do what he likes.

Because that's a line I will absolutely never cross.

He's safe with me. He probably flirts like breathing, and knowing that I won't use that against him hopefully makes him feel secure. He can woo me and everyone around us because if we're honest, that's how most people get ahead in this industry.

But I'll be with him on this venture to make sure no one takes advantage of him like I have no doubt Chris did.

He shakes himself and smiles as he picks the menu back up and scans the page. "The set meal looks divine," he purrs. "I suppose I could allow you to treat me a little."

I'm going to treat him a lot. Like I told myself earlier, there's no real harm in that.

"In that case, you won't mind me ordering Champagne, either," I say mischievously as I catch the eye of our waitress.

He bites his lip again, but he's not coy this time. He's positively gleeful. "Well, we *are* celebrating, aren't we, sweetie? It would be rude not to."

He looks me up and down like he could happily devour me instead of the food we're about to order. I'm not sure if he's just playing or he's genuinely interested now that it's on his terms and he's not being pressured into anything.

I tell myself it's irrelevant. I can take it as a compliment, but it's not going to lead to anything. Because it can't. I've made him my responsibility. So I'm going to look after him no matter what.

Even if he's so delicious I could lick him like a plate.

5

———

MALYK

It's not like I've never been on a plane before. Mum and I went on a few cheap package holidays as a kid, not to mention I've been on a couple of gay singles holidays over the years to Gran Canaria and the like.

But there's flying, and then there's flying *first class*.

I had no idea what Oscar even meant by a lounge, but apparently, it's like a members-only club that *I* was allowed into, and then everything in there was *free!* Including the booze! I didn't want to appear greedy, but Oscar casually filled up a plate of food from the buffet and grabbed a beer before giving me a pointed look, so you can bet your arse I did the same, except with a glass of Champagne because apparently since I met him, I've become bougie.

We're on the plane now, and I won't lie—I was a little worried about being stuck in a small seat with my giraffe legs for an eight-hour flight. That's a lot longer than what I'm used to. But these seats are *huge*—like our own comfy bed pods—and all the food and drink is *still* free.

I keep getting flashes of guilt, thinking how much this all must have cost. How did I end up the lucky one here? Out of all the models on that shoot—hell, everyone I know in London would kill for this opportunity. And yet I'm the one who's sitting pretty, just because my ex decided to be a petty bitch.

But when I doubt it all, I make myself recall what Oscar said to me over dinner the other night. He thinks I have real potential. He sees something in me. And he's a man who knows what he's talking about. So I force myself to remember that and trust it.

Besides, with the Champagne flowing freely, I can't deny that I'm having *fun*.

It helps that the company is good. Once Oscar assured me that he wasn't expecting you-know-what in exchange for this kind act, it became a lot easier to flirt with him. I know I'm being stupid. He's so mature and experienced that he'd never be interested in a silly thing like me. Unfortunately, that just makes him hotter to me.

I like the way he never runs out of stories of the wild people he's met and knows in this industry. But what I like even more is that he never tells a joke at anyone's expense. He's never mean or laughing *at* people in these tall tales. It's always with them or at himself. Like the time he accidentally found himself at an orgy but decided to stay because the shrimp was really good.

I laughed so hard I almost choked at that one. I keep waiting for him to tell me to quieten down or be more demure, especially as we're in public. But he just watches me with that same delight he's had since we met.

I tell myself it's nothing. That he just sees potential in me as a model.

He doesn't fancy me.

I'm such a child with my nose pressed up against the window as we take off. I always love that swoopy tummy feeling when the plane revs up and finally races into the air after a long taxi. London disappears beneath the early morning clouds, and I realize this is really it.

No going back now.

It's not long until the seat belt sign dings off, and I've got another glass of Champagne in my hand. Even though we ate at the airport, the cabin crew are already coming around with a little tray filled with pastries, jam, and butter.

"Urgh, here we go," Oscar groans once the flight attendant is out of earshot. "The never-ending parade of food."

I scoff and rip into a warm, fluffy croissant. "You say that like it's a bad thing." I grin and slather butter onto half of it, then wash it down with a sip of delicious bubbles.

Oscar drinks his black coffee and looks warmly at me like the way he was doing the other night at dinner. Like he thinks I'm cute. Normally I'd prefer to be thought of as fierce, but for him, I quite like being cute. He's safe like that.

God, when did I become such a loser? When did 'safe' become sexier than 'mysterious' or 'dangerous'?

Probably right around the time Chris cheated on me and added himself to the long list of arseholes I've wasted my time on over the years.

"Ah, to be young and still have a metabolism," Oscar says wistfully, that twinkle back in his hazel eyes.

"You're not old," I protest, finishing off the rest of the croissant.

I have to admit that I'm still pretty full from the lounge food, so I take a break from the other nibbles for now and knock back the glass of juice that came with the breakfast. It's a long flight, and I need to be careful I don't booze my way through it and have to be carried off.

"I'm not young anymore, either," Oscar says fondly.

I frown. "How old are you?" I ask.

"Forty-two," he says.

I laugh. "That's not old," I tell him firmly. "Especially these days. Nobody I know seems to have their shit together until at *least* their mid-thirties. Hey!" I add as I realize something. "We're opposite! I'm twenty-four."

He chuckles from across the small aisle in his cozy pod. "So young."

I pretend to flick my hair and preen, trying not to show that I'm disappointed he basically thinks of me as a child. I already knew that, but still, I've had a couple of glasses of Champagne now and am feeling cocky. Or cocky-*er* than usual, I should say.

"She's old enough to know a thing or two, I'll have you know." I flutter my eyelashes at him and sip my drink, hoping he gets what kinds of things I mean. "I left school at sixteen. I'm not sheltered. I know how to work hard *and* play hard."

"I don't doubt it," Oscar murmurs.

He holds my gaze just long enough for my skin to start getting warm and prickly, but then he reaches into his bag and pulls out a pen and small notepad. "Okay, so you're twenty-four. When's your birthday?"

"March twenty-fifth," I reply automatically. "An Aries, of course. Why?"

I watch him make a note. "If we're going to pretend to be dating, it seems prudent to get some key details down."

I blink. Oh…*shit*. Yeah. That's how this whole thing started in front of Chris. I'd been so busy flirting I'd completely forgotten.

"Oh, we don't have to do that if you don't want to," I say, feeling embarrassed for some reason. I've been teasing him, yeah, but he seemed to be enjoying it. After me checking in with his expectations, I don't want *him* thinking *I* expect anything in return.

He shrugs. "It seems sensible to keep up the charade if Oakley is going to be there," he says like it's no big deal. "Plus, Emmalina is going to want to know why *this* year I finally caved and brought someone, so this seems the obvious answer."

"One," I say, holding up my index finger feeling agitated, "I thought you were bringing me because you thought I had a lot of potential. And two, does that mean you don't normally date? Like…ever?"

I know he's been going to this retreat basically since

it started a decade ago. Has he never brought someone along before?

"You do have potential," Oscar assures me, which calms me down a little. "But Emmalina loves gossip, so she'll be far more interested in you if she thinks you're my boy toy. So we might as well continue the pretense we started with Oakley. It's only a small white lie, no harm."

I shrug. I don't love lying, but I guess it'll be more like me flirting like usual and then not correcting anyone's assumptions as to what our relationship is. I'm not going to be inventing any sordid details to spread around or anything. We can hold hands for a week, I'm sure. If so, it would make sense to know more about each other in case anyone gets nosy.

"And?" I prompt.

"And what?" he says with a frown.

I laugh. "Don't avoid the question. Honeyrock has been going on for ten years. You're telling me you weren't dating that whole time?"

He sighs and narrows his eyes a bit, but I don't think I've really crossed a line. Just been a healthy amount of bratty.

"I dated," he says eventually once the cabin crew has taken our trays away. "Jerry was a lab technician, though. He couldn't have had less interest in a weeklong party with models and fashion designers."

There's something bitter in his voice. It pains me, but I get the immediate feeling that this Jerry looked down on the industry Oscar works in.

Don't get me wrong—we spent *most* of our dinner

bitching about models and the like. But it's our world. We get to do that because in the end, we love it.

Did Jerry belittle Oscar Wainwright, by far the greatest photographer I've had the pleasure of working with in my career to date?

"How long were you together?" I ask evenly.

He shrugs. "A little over three years. For a while, I thought he was the one. Even considered proposing. But ultimately, we wanted different things. And he never liked my dog."

I gasp so loud the nearest flight attendant looks around in concern. I give her a reassuring smile and shake my head to show I'm okay before returning my rapt attention to Oscar.

"He didn't like your *dog?* You *have* a dog?"

He chuckles and unlocks his phone, quickly pulling up a photo of a caramel-colored teddy bear with a lolling pink tongue as well as black eyes and nose. I squeal and make grabbing motions with my fingers until he hands the phone over and lets me zoom in on the pooch's face.

"Oh my *goddd,* what a cutie," I groan. "What's their name? How old are they?"

Oscar laughs louder. "Is it me you're pretending to date or the dog?" he teases, but I can tell he's pleased. And I was correct. Jerry was obviously a wanker if he did anything less than absolutely adore this angel. "His name is Samson—because of his hair. He's a labradoodle, and he's nine."

That's getting a bit old for a dog, but I don't let that

diminish my excitement at all. He looks like he's got a good few more years left in him yet.

"Well, you've got competition," I announce as I hand Oscar his phone back. "Samson looks like a *very* good boy and has already stolen my heart, I'm afraid."

Oscar smiles and rubs his thumb against the side of his phone. I pretend not to notice in an attempt to stop myself from shivering. I'm just infatuated with him because he's nice and he's got his shit together. That's rare in the blokes I usually meet. Just because I'm imagining what those strong fingers would feel like caressing against my skin doesn't mean anything.

"He's the best boy," Oscar says with a deep affection as he looks down at his screen.

I get it. Mum and I had a dog when I was growing up. Bertie. No idea what breed he was—he was a rescue and probably had ten mixes in him—but he was the kindest soul I ever met, and I cried for weeks when he passed away. Dogs are brilliant, and as soon as I get a place that allows pets, I'm off to rescue one of my own.

"Okay, so now I know the most important thing about you," I say playfully, gesturing to the phone to indicate Samson. "Is there anything else?"

He laughs and pockets the mobile. "You're right, that is the most important thing. I guess I should mention I've lived in New York since I graduated from college."

"I've never been," I say in wonder. "Did you live at home before that?"

He nods. "With my parents and younger sister in a little town just outside Columbus, Ohio."

"Are you close?" I ask with a raised eyebrow. I feel like I'm interrogating him, but he's smiling, so I know I'm not annoying him. It's fun getting a glimpse into his life.

"I call them about once a month and go home for the holidays," he says with a shrug. "Not super close but not estranged either. How about you?"

I also shrug. "It's just me and Mum. Dad left when I was a baby, wanker. I grew up near Newport—that's in Wales, near the English border. We managed okay. I got my GCSEs and decided that was enough of formal education, so I worked in shops and restaurants and stuff."

I waggle my eyebrows, not wanting the dwell on those really tough years and get to the good stuff.

"I was bullied all throughout school for being too tall and skinny, but then something happened as I approached my twenties, and I went from gawky to gorgeous almost overnight. *That's* when I discovered the magic of Instagram. Fifty thousand followers just because I was good at taking selfies? What a lark. Companies started sending me stuff to model for them, and I got a taste of it."

A little *too* much of a taste for it. Oscar doesn't need to know that I'm still paying—literally—for how young and stupid I was. This industry is so superficial, though. I was convinced I couldn't ever wear the same clothes twice and everything had to be designer. I witnessed so many people get canceled for the most ridiculous things like that and as far as I saw it, modeling was my only way out of the small, homophobic town I was stuck in.

I wasn't going back to being that bullied little kid who cried himself to sleep. I gave it everything I had and then some.

I've promised myself I'm not allowed another credit card until I've paid off all my debts. I'm sure it'll take years, but I'm determined to do it. And I'll do it before Mum ever finds out what trouble I got myself into. I couldn't bear the shame of her knowing I let her down like that. She raised me right. I just let the superficial side of this cutthroat industry warp my young mind.

I push down the embarrassment I feel at those memories and focus instead on my triumph. "When I hit seventy thousand followers, I started applying to agencies, and after a while I got signed with McKay's. It was the best day of my life."

I grin, remembering how Mum and I had cried. We'd splashed out on a Chinese takeaway and a bottle of real Champagne. I look at the glass in my hand now and imagine what I might be telling her in a week or two. I haven't even told her I'm going away. I don't want to get her hopes up, because if it all goes to shit, that'll devastate me twice as much.

Hopefully, I'll be able to go home with *two* bottles of Champagne this time. I just have to play my cards right.

And that means I need to stop lusting after Oscar and keep things professional. If I can catch this lucky break, I might be able to pay off all my foolish debts and start fresh. This could be the beginning of a completely new chapter in my life.

I have to think with my head, not my heart. Or other body parts, if you catch my drift.

"Are you going to be posting online while you're away?" Oscar asks, sounding genuinely curious.

I shake my head. "I'll film plenty of B roll and take photos, but I won't post anything unless something comes of it. I don't want to jinx anything."

I take a look at the free bag of luxury toiletries they've given us, and am already thinking of doing an unpacking vid. There's some seriously cute stuff in there. It's hard coming up with new content ideas all the time, so I'm excited by the idea of something really different that I think my viewers would enjoy.

"Can I get you gentlemen another drink?" the flight attendant asks.

I glance at Oscar. He's already insisted several times that everything is included and I should have what I want, but I still feel like I want to check in with him. I get a thrill as he answers the guy for us. "Two glasses of Champagne," he says with a grin. "We're celebrating."

"We are!" I agree with a laugh. Once we have our glasses, I suggest taking a selfie to capture the moment. "I guess it'll probably be good to have some coupley photos as well," I say. "Just in case anyone asks."

"Good thinking," he murmurs with a smile, leaning in for the photo.

I smile back at him, my heart fluttering, then quickly take the picture and allow the moment to pass. He might be off-limits, but that doesn't mean we can't raise a glass to this fantastical scheme of ours.

I'm going to spend the next several hours learning

all I can about my new 'boyfriend.' Then I'm going to spend the next several days on his arm, charming some of the most important people on the East Coast fashion scene.

I'm going to make my mum proud.

6

OSCAR

"Malyk?" I call out as he starts wandering off from the luggage belt once he's gotten his bag. "This way," I say warmly. I know the JFK airport like the back of my hand, but I can see how easy it would be to get turned around on your first visit.

He frowns and points to one of the signs overhead. "But it says the train and subway is this direction."

Oh, bless him. Apparently, he does have a clue where he's going. He's still going the wrong way, though.

I bump shoulders with him and take his suitcase handle with my free hand. "You're right," I say mysteriously, then lead him the opposite way.

He catches up with me after a few seconds, which isn't surprising, considering how long his legs are. He glances at me in confusion but doesn't say anything until we get outside to the taxi rank.

"But that's…!" he starts to protest. 'Too expensive' was undoubtedly the end of that sentence, but he sensibly swallows it. Good. He's getting the hang of how this trip is going to work, and I just grin at him.

"That's a car that's going to take us all the way to the front of my apartment building, yes," I say playfully. "We've both been stuck in a tin can for the best part of eight hours. I'm not going to get into another one if I don't have to."

He nods as we join the line. There are half a dozen people in front of us, but as with everything in this city, they're moving fast. Normally, I'd organize a private car hire, but I don't tend to from the airport in case the plane is delayed. A cab will do the job just as well in this instance.

"They're real yellow cabs," he says in the lilting accent that I now know is a mixture of Welsh and the melting pot of London. "I had a toy one of those when I was a lad."

"I'd have thought you'd have been more of a Barbie boy." I chuckle and wink at him so he knows I'm only teasing. He scrunches up his nose. It's adorable.

"Not when my dad was around, but after he buggered off, Mum let me buy anything. It was usually from the pound shop, so cheap as chips, but I had dolls and cars and dinosaurs and tea sets—you name it. She didn't give a shit."

"Sounds like a good mom," I say genuinely.

His returning smile is equally authentic. "The best. One day, I'll be mega rich and buy her a house, and she'll never have to work again."

"That's a solid plan," I tell him sincerely. It doesn't pass me by that his dream is to take care of *her.* I'm sure that he'll want things for himself if he's successful, but I like that he hasn't forgotten the only true family he has.

For a crazy second, I get the idea that he could buy his mom a place, and *I* could buy *him* a place. Fuck me. It's one thing to have organized a plane ticket and an exclusive invitation. It's quite another to picture surprising him with something so extravagant as a *house.*

It's just guilt. I'm sitting on more money than I know what to do with. It's probably only natural that I'd think about sharing it with a new friend who's in a completely different financial situation.

Obviously, buying a house outright is a huge amount of money. But I could probably give him enough for a down payment and not think twice, whereas it would be life changing for him.

I shake my head, dismissing the crazy thoughts as it's our turn to get in a cab, and I help our driver put the bags in the trunk. I know I'm jetlagged and still buzzing a little from indulging on the plane, but I need to calm down. I never normally drink while flying, but being with Malyk made me feel kind of reckless. When was the last time I let loose and had some real fun?

Too long, according to Jerry.

It was weird discussing him, but I'm glad I did. Normally, talking about myself feels pretty awkward, but not with Malyk. He soaked up all my words like I was giving a fascinating seminar on his favorite subject.

It's a bit dangerous how much I'm enjoying basking in his glow.

What's more dangerous is the way I catch the cabbie staring at Malyk in the rearview mirror as I slide into the backseat. I know the guy probably can't help it. My new friend is absolutely stunning. But he's also *mine*. I have to protect him. So before we even pull away from the curb, I wrap my arm around his slim shoulders and take one of his hands in my free one.

He looks at me in shock, but I raise my eyebrows. "Practice, remember?" I murmur low enough that I hope I won't be heard over the rumble of the engine or the radio playing up front.

"Oh," he puffs out and relaxes with a nod. We'd discussed practicing PDA before we got to the retreat so it wouldn't feel strange and possibly give us away. "Sure. This is nice."

He snuggles against me like we're a regular couple who are tired after a long flight. I shouldn't be so smug that the cabbie keeps his eyes on the road after that, but I am.

Damn. I suppose it's different because Malyk is literally model good looking, and the vultures feel like they're always circling around him, but I'm not sure I've ever felt like this about a guy. Like I have to beat my chest and roar to warn other men away. Because he's *mine*.

Except he's not. Of course he's not. I'm just getting carried away.

Traffic is pretty okay for once, and we make it into Manhattan within an hour. Malyk falls asleep against me. I let him, seeing as he'll have to wake up once we get to my place. A little nap might help him make it through the rest of the afternoon and evening. He's only got a day to adjust to a new time zone, as we have to head to the retreat tomorrow. I'm so used to flying I know I'll be able to suck it up and work through the fog until a decent time tonight. But for now, I just watch him sleeping peacefully.

"We're here," I say gently as our driver pulls up to the curb. He can't wait long, so I tap my card to his meter, then rub Malyk's thigh again. "Wake up, sweetie."

He blinks lashes that are so long they grace his cheekbones. People pay good money for that, yet he has it naturally. He really is a star waiting to be born, but I'm not convinced he really believes that yet.

I can't wait to show him.

I'm going to show him so much while he's here in the Big Apple. Once he's woken up and extracted himself from the cab, he looks up at all the high-rises with his mouth open.

"It's not like we don't have tall buildings in London," he clarifies as I retrieve our bags from the driver, who's pulled them from the trunk. "But I get what people mean about *skyscrapers* now." The thud of the trunk closing brings his attention back down. "Cheers, mate," he says to the cabbie with a wave.

The cabbie nods back but, after glancing at me, he hurries back into his car and pulls away.

Malyk doesn't seem to notice. Instead, he tries to reach for his case, but I grab both the handles and haul my and his bags toward the front door. "Nice try," I gloat.

He huffs and dashes to my side again. "I can manage my own bag, you know."

"But if you were really my boyfriend, you wouldn't have to," I tell him with a wink.

His skin is a little darker than mine, but I can still tell he's blushing. I probably shouldn't be flirting like that, but he makes it so impossible not to.

I say hi to Mo, the building's doorman, and collect the mail that's piled up for me since I've been away. Malyk doesn't say anything as we ride the elevator up to my floor. It's not the penthouse, but it's certainly high enough for me.

I hear the whining and barking before I even get my key out.

Malyk goes from looking like a zombie to dancing on his tiptoes as he waits for me to open my door. "Puppy, puppy, puppy," he chants with his fists balled up in front of his chest.

Jerry only ever tolerated Samson. Malyk's enthusiasm is…dangerous…for my resolve. So I turn away and instead focus on ensuring that my four-legged floor mop doesn't come bursting out of the apartment and tackle me to the floor.

Except it's not me he bombards.

Well, I get a brief sniff, but then it's Malyk he jumps up for, much to my horror.

"Samson, no! Down!" I cry, but Malyk has dropped to his knees in the damn hallway and is letting my beast slobber all over him.

"Hello, gorgeous boy!" he coos, ruffling either side of Sam's face. "Who's a good baby? It's you!"

He doesn't care that his nice clothes are getting hair all over him or that Sam's breath leaves something to be desired. He throws his arms around my dog's neck like they're long-lost buddies, and hugs him tightly without a care in the world.

My throat gets tight. I thought he was beautiful before, but that…

I clear my throat. *Off-limits!* I remind myself.

"We should probably get inside," I say gently.

Malyk laughs and shoos Samson inside my apartment before climbing back to his feet and following.

It's been a very long time since anyone was in my home, aside from me or my dog. I have friends, but I meet them at bars or for dinner. The few hook-ups I've indulged in have been at someone else's place or hotels. So it suddenly feels very real once I drag the cases inside and close the door behind me. Malyk is actually here, and he's looking around in awe.

"This is lush," he says approvingly.

It is nice to show my place off for once, and it's interesting seeing my home through fresh eyes. I have several of my favorite-ever snaps framed on the walls. A lot of the furniture is custom, and I worked with an interior designer to get a quirky, modern feeling that wasn't too abstract or cold. The monochrome tones that run through the apartment are broken up with splashes of bright colors from a rug or a lamp.

"Thank you," I murmur.

I don't know why it's important to me that he genuinely likes my home, but it is. Thankfully, it seems he does from the way he's twirling around and beaming.

I clear my throat to stop myself from staring yet again. "Let's set you up in the guest bedroom," I suggest. He looks back at me, and I indicate the room to my left where he'll be staying tonight. Tomorrow, we'll head to Honeyrock, but for now, we can freshen up and unwind until the morning.

"Thanks," he says with a sigh. He's probably exhausted, but I'm going to have to try and keep him awake if I can.

I resolutely ignore the suggestion my brain supplies. What the hell is wrong with me? He's half my age! The flirting is nice—flattering, even—but he doesn't mean it. He doesn't have a crush on me. He's just being friendly.

"Are you hungry?" I ask as I haul his suitcase onto the bed for him.

He hums. "Strangely…kind of, yes," he says. "You were right about the plane food being non-stop, but the last snack was a couple of hours ago now. I wouldn't mind something this evening before bed."

I nod. "Why don't we go for a walk? There's a small park nearby with a dog-friendly Italian place on the corner. We can sit outside and watch the birds a while to keep us awake."

He opens his mouth to reply but a yawn catches him off guard. Once he shakes it off, he laughs. "Yeah, a walk sounds like a good way to prevent from passing out," he admits.

"I'll give you fifteen minutes to freshen up," I say as I back out of the door.

I need the same, and eagerly drag my case over to the main bedroom with Samson in tow, wagging his tail like this is the best day of his life. I had a neighbor come in every day to feed and walk him, but he's a social creature and is used to having me home most of the time.

"You missed Daddy, huh?" I say as I change into fresh clothes and find my deodorant. He watches me, his tail never stopping and his dark eyes wide and excited. "You want to come with us? Get to know Daddy's new friend?"

He barks, and I take that as a yes.

The dangerous thing about walking around a cute park with my dog and a seriously hot guy, then going to dinner, is that it feels extremely coupley. We said we were going to practice PDA, so we even hold hands, and I notice several appreciative looks and smiles that are sent our way.

This isn't real, though. It's not a date. It's just a necessity for keeping my new friend awake. And fed. For someone so skinny, he eats a lot. So I'm just being responsible.

That's what I also tell myself as I get him home a couple of hours later and practically have to carry him into his bed. He's dead on his feet and mumbling sweetly—not to me, of course. But to my damned dog. I have to laugh at how easily they've bonded.

"I'll leave the door ajar," I promise him after he's brushed his teeth. "If you need anything, just call out. I'll hear."

He blinks sleepily at me, then smiles. "I will. Thank you, Oscar."

I hesitate just a bit too long, wanting to ask if he needs anything else. Then I remind myself that he's an adult and is more than capable of taking care of himself.

I put a load of laundry on and repack some of my case for the week ahead. I always knew it would be a little tight doing two trips back to back, but nothing I can't handle.

What I really can't handle is knowing that Malyk is just across the hall. I try not to think about how much I want to curl up behind him and fall asleep with him in my arms. It's crazy. I'd have never called myself protective before, but now it's like I think I'm all that's going to stand between him and a world that wants to hurt him.

When I finally crawl into bed, I expect sleep to claim me quickly. But I just end up staring at the ceiling for what feels like hours. It doesn't help that Samson has abandoned me as well. Usually, after a trip, he's glued to my side, but tonight he's left me all alone.

Well…if I *am* all alone…

Jerking off always helps me sleep. It's a fact. That's the only reason I lick my palm and reach under the sheets to take myself in hand. I keep quiet, as my door is slightly open, and try not to think of anything other than how good my palm feels against my hardening cock. I certainly don't think of light, bright eyes or long fingers that could be the ones stroking me right now.

I grit my teeth, the orgasm hitting me surprisingly fast. I manage to get most of the mess on my hand at least, and when I've come back to my senses, I grab some tissues to stop the sheets from getting sticky. I sigh as I wad them up and toss them into the trash can.

I didn't exactly cross a line. And I'm only human. I

have needs. But I'm going to have to be real careful over this next week.

If I'm going to make it my mission to protect Malyk, that includes protecting him from me.

I can't give in to this temptation.

7

MALYK

My dreams are very weird that night. I guess it's because of the long flight, new surroundings, a good amount of booze mixed with non-stop food, also being in a completely different time zone. But I dream of my old house, school, and work, and the details are a little fuzzy, but there's definitely something sexy going on.

I wake up at around five, and it's still dark out. My hard-on is almost painful, so I need to do something about it, but it feels really wrong to toss off in someone else's guest bed. So I make a snap decision and grab my wash kit and the towel Oscar left me before nipping into the bathroom for a much-needed shower and an even more necessary wank.

I bite my lip and try not to groan as my hand flies over my throbbing shaft. Fuck, whatever that dream was, it was certainly fruity. I press my other palm against the wall tiles to give myself some purchase, letting the scalding hot water flow over my trembling body.

I try not to give a face to the man I picture behind me, pressing up against my back and kissing my neck as he brings me to my climax. But he's older, and his big cock is rubbing against my bum as he nibbles my earlobe and mumbles my name.

"Oscar," I grunt before I can help myself, and then I'm spurting all over my hand and into the bottom of the shower.

It seems to last for ages, and then it takes a minute or two for me to come down from the high. Guilt creeps in. He's been so bloody nice to me, and here I am, perving over him. Well, I suppose it's *because* he's been so nice that I pictured such a tender moment between us. I've never actually had shower sex, but I bet Oscar has. He seems like the kind of bloke who'd take gentle care of his partner post-fucking.

Whoever that partner might be.

No, I'm not going to feel bad about this. I'm only human and jetlagged. Besides, it's just a naughty fantasy. No one on earth ever needs to know about it—certainly not Oscar. I'm just crushing on him because he's been so lovely. Not to mention that our relationship so far has been brief but incredibly intense. I'll soon calm down and get back to normal, I'm sure.

I sigh with relief as the water washes the last evidence of my orgasm away, then take my time cleaning my body and hair. I try to be as quiet as I can so as not to disturb Oscar, but when I open the door several minutes later, Samson is lying in wait for me. As soon as he sees me, he jumps to his feet, his tail wagging as he whines and whimpers in delight.

"Shh, shh," I beg him, waving my hands. I glance toward Oscar's room, but I don't hear him stirring. So I look back down at Samson. "Do you need to go out?" I whisper.

He runs to the door and looks back at me. Therefore, I take that as a yes. I don't want to wake Oscar, so I get the apartment and building keys from the bowl on the table in the hall and shove my feet into my trainers, not caring that I'm still in my pajamas. I couldn't be bothered to find new clothes in my still-packed suitcase, and fully intend on getting back into bed. Oscar's neighbors are just going to have to deal with my state of undress if they see me. I'm still wearing a T-shirt and trousers, just nothing underneath.

Oh, what the hell? This is New York. I'm *not* going to be the strangest sight anyone sees today.

Samson used a small grassy area just outside the building last night when we came home after dinner, so I lead him there to do his business and quickly clear it up. He runs around a bit like he wants to play, but I haven't got a ball with me or anything. Plus, I'm starting to shiver as dawn is only just creeping over the horizon. Mercifully, he does come after I call him a few times, and we head back up to Oscar's flat.

It's only when I'm in the elevator that I realize how intimate we already are. I don't have any friends in London that I've stayed the night with in a non-sexy way, and I certainly wouldn't have the confidence to take charge of any of their pets without asking. It's like Oscar and I are already in a relationship.

Except we're not, and I need to remember that.

I crawl back into bed with a happy groan, prepared to fall asleep again right away. I laugh when Samson hops up and joins me. "Are you allowed up here?" I whisper, not having checked the rules with Oscar. But Samson just turns in a circle and plops down by my legs, his eyes already closed, so I guess that settles that. Bertie used to sleep on my bed as a kid, so as I drift back off to sleep, I'm not surprised that I dream pleasantly of him.

This time, I'm woken up by the amazing smell of bacon and coffee. It's fully bright now behind the blinds, and Samson is gone from the bed. I stretch and crack my neck before venturing out into the rest of the apartment.

"Cheeky boy," I scoff when I see Samson waiting at Oscar's feet as he makes breakfast. For a second, Oscar whips his head around with wide eyes. But then he looks down and realizes I was talking to his dog, and laughs.

Interesting. Maybe I should try and call *him* a cheeky boy later.

No! Bad Malyk. Stop that.

"Morning," Oscar says a little too cheerfully. He's in jeans and a T-shirt, and I'm glad that I wore long pajama bottoms instead of booty shorts. There's something slightly charged and awkward in the air.

This fake-dating thing will hopefully get better when there are other people around. Because right now, we're sort of pretending just for ourselves, and it's making me wonder where the boundaries actually lie.

"Sleep well?" Oscar asks.

I nod and sit at the breakfast bar. "And I showered. I hope that's okay?"

"Of course," he says, starting to plate a fair bit of food up. "Thanks for letting Samson out. I notice he slept with you, the traitor."

He grins as he brings the food over to me, and I gasp. There's bacon, fried eggs, and a little stack of pancakes all covered with maple syrup and melting butter. "Wow," I say, taken aback. "This is so nice, thank you."

"Welcome to America," he says with a wink. "I'm afraid I don't have any tea. Can I interest you in coffee?"

"Caffeine sounds good for today," I admit as I cut into the bacon, which is far crispier than we have back home. "So long as there's sugar."

"And cream," he affirms, placing a cup of rich-smelling liquid in front of me as well as the condiment jars.

"This is amazing," I say around a mouthful of fluffy, sweet pancakes. "But tell me you had a proper fry-up in London. With baked beans and black pudding."

He crinkles his nose, and I laugh. "I can't say I'm a fan of black pudding," he confesses as he gets his own plate and stands in front of me on the other side of the bar. "But I'm a fan of what you guys call baked beans."

I raise an eyebrow. "What do you call them?"

He shrugs. "We don't. They don't really exist over here. What we call baked beans are different."

"Huh," I say with a nod. "You'll have to show me."

"I will," he says warmly.

I'm already enjoying discovering all these differences

between the two countries. But it does remind me just how different Oscar and I are culturally as well as in age. Still, it's not completely alien to me. It's just going to take some getting used to.

I stab at a bit of egg white and internally roll my eyes. For the last time, we're not *really* dating. I don't have to get used to the culture shock because in a week I'll be heading back home to where everything is familiar.

"So the drive's about an hour," Oscar says as he sips his coffee. I've ladened mine with cream and sugar, but he's just having his black again. It is good stuff that's come from a fresh pot, much nicer than the instant granules I'm familiar with back home. Perhaps I could get used to coffee after all.

"When do you want to leave?" I ask, suddenly nervous.

I talk a lot of shit, but I am actually going to have to impress these people if I don't want it to be a wasted journey. And Chris is going to be there. I don't want to embarrass myself in front of him, either.

I thought I was putting on a brave face, but Oscar reaches out and covers my hand with his own, rubbing his thumb against my skin in a comforting way. A shiver runs down my spine, and I look up into his hazel eyes.

"You're going to be amazing," he assures me like he could read my thoughts.

I chew my lip. It's sweet from the syrup. "Am I?" I ask. "I don't even know what I'm supposed to do."

He shrugs and lets go of me. I miss the contact immediately, but it's probably for the best. "Just be yourself," he says, like it's that easy. "Get involved. Don't be a wallflower. But don't be a dick, either. Not that I think you would be. It's just that Emmalina sees through bullshit in a heartbeat."

I scoff. "So how's she going to believe we're dating?" I say with a nervous laugh.

"We'll just have to be extra convincing," Oscar says with a wink.

Oh, my lord.

How am I ever going to survive this week?

8

———

MALYK

Westchester is twenty miles north of Manhattan, I've discovered. Once again, we take a cab because Oscar doesn't own a car. I get it. No one I know in London owns one either. Traffic is a nightmare, and affording a place with parking is ludicrous. But that's why I know the Tube and buses like the back of my hand. It would never occur to me to book a taxi, especially not two days in a row, *especially* when both journeys are over an hour long each.

But Oscar doesn't bat an eyelid, so I don't comment. He doesn't seem to like me protesting about him spending money, and I don't want to come across as a skinflint. I'm just so used to being poor it's taking quite a bit of effort for me to relax and enjoy the luxury.

This taxi isn't a yellow cab, either. It's a sleek black private hire with complimentary bottled water and packets of pretzels for us in the back seat. He paid extra for a dog-friendly service, and Samson is sleeping peacefully at our feet. There's even a darkened partition between us and the driver, which makes me a little nervous.

It's getting harder and harder to be alone with Oscar and ignore these feelings bubbling up inside me. I glance at him beside me, taking in his slightly smarter appearance compared to how I've seen him until now. The baseball cap has gone, and he's tidied up his beard. He's still wearing jeans that cling to his arse and thighs, but now he's paired them with a button-down instead of a polo shirt. He's currently lost in thought, looking out the window, his elbow leaning against the door as he rubs his chin.

Damn. Someone should take a photo of *that*.

"So is there an itinerary or something for this week?" I ask to distract myself as we drive north.

He blinks and smiles at me. "I suppose I should finally look at that email Emmalina sent to me months ago," he says with that twinkle in his eyes. I'm not surprised he's so chill about it. That's just who he is.

I would have memorized the entire contents of that message weeks ago.

"It's mostly themed parties and games and such," Oscar says with a shrug. He looks down at his phone screen as he scrolls. "Just one long networking event. Emmalina likes to think of all her people as family, so this is kind of like a reunion."

I don't really have a frame of reference for family reunions other than what I've seen in movies and television. I think of romcom hijinks where sons and fathers fight about who's going to take over the family business or who should marry who. I suppose what we're doing with this fake boyfriends scheme is like something straight out of a script.

I don't know if that makes me more or less nervous.

"Hmm, I can't find the exact email," Oscar says, giving up and pocketing his phone. "But the first evening is always a big mixer by the pool—not *in* the pool, though. That will be tomorrow during the day. No doubt Linny will have hired some hip DJ that the kids are into and have professional dancers on podiums. There's usually a fireworks display."

He talks about it all so casually like this woman isn't throwing a full-blown rave in her back garden. I'd heard of her before, but obviously I've looked her up online since this whole caper began. Her brand is definitely a quirky kind of couture, which I have to say I love. I'm drawn to more unusual styles. As much as I complained to myself about the uncomfortableness of the shoot the other day, I actually really vibed with the whole fairy theme. The Emmalina aesthetic typically has a load of skulls, roses, birds, and chains with bold colors and asymmetric jewelry.

The idea of stomping down the runway at one of their shows leaves me weak at the knees.

But I'm getting ahead of myself. First, I've got to meet the woman, let alone impress her. Then I can go about maybe convincing her that I'm the kind of model who would suit their image well.

I can only be so lucky.

Oscar starts talking about the kinds of people that will be there. Other photographers like himself, models who are already representing the line, and hopefuls like me, agents, other designers, and personal friends of Emmalina. It sounds like it's going to be a packed house for sure. Not everybody stays on-site, apparently, although she does have an entire building of guest quarters just for that purpose. Some choose to stay in town, and others only come for one day of events before jetting off again.

The realization that some of these people probably fly on private jets makes my head swim.

We drive through a quaint little town—the kind with a clock tower in the center and a general store that's probably been owned by the same family for over three generations. There are plenty of trees along the streets with lush green leaves, and I can tell the schools are still on summer holidays because teenagers are walking everywhere in gaggles or rushing along on rollerblades and bikes.

It all feels pretty wholesome. Not my usual scene. I come from a much tougher little town that had a somewhat suffocating air to it. Like a kettle that was always on the brink of boiling over. This feels joyful. Peaceful.

We head back out into the countryside, where the houses are few and far between, before arriving at a perimeter fence with tall trees towering behind it. The road leads to a grand double gate that we pause in front of. Our driver rolls down the window to speak into an intercom, but because of the partition, I can't really hear what he says.

"I'm guessing this is Honeyrock," I say to Oscar with my eyes fixed on the gates as they start to slowly swing open. I try not to let nerves make my voice shake, and slip my trembling hands under my thighs.

Am I delusional?

What the hell makes me think I can fit in with these people? They're sophisticated, educated, well-traveled, and, not to mention, mega rich. I am on the *wrong* side of the tracks. Never mind the whole pretending to date Oscar bullshit. One look at me and they're going to send me back to my council estate where I belong.

Oscar's hand slips over my thigh, and I can't help the little gasp that escapes. I try and cover it up by biting my lower lip as I look over at him.

"You've got nothing to be nervous about," he murmurs, rubbing my leg with his thumb. Shivers run down my spine. "You're my guest, and you have every right to be here. They're going to love you. You're going to shine like a star."

I swallow and hold his gaze. For a really stupid second, I get bratty and wonder why Oscar *can't* be my boyfriend. He's already so good at it.

But then I remember that would be a monumentally bad idea. Look what happened the last time I mixed work with a relationship. Chris has been trying to starve me out of work and very nearly stopped me from coming here. Nope. I promised myself that I wouldn't ever date anyone from the industry again. I'm not even going to risk sex. I've got an incredible opportunity here, and I'm not going to squander it by thinking with my dick.

"Thank you," I say warmly. I remove my hands from

under my thighs and use one to squeeze his back. "For everything."

He grins and juts his chin toward the window. *"Now we're here."*

While I've been fretting, the car has made its way down the winding driveway, also lined with trees. This place must be hidden away in an actual forest. I feel like I'm a princess in a fairy tale. I guess in a way, I am. Just a poor girl who's been whisked off to the castle to see the queen with a handsome knight in shining armor by her side.

Not every fairy tale has to end with a royal wedding. Look at Frozen. I can be strong, independent, and successful, and that will be the scene the credits roll on.

Not with me in Oscar's arms, and that's fine.

Samson must sense that we're slowing down because he lifts his head with a big yawn, then rises to his feet. Oscar and I both laugh as the big lump of a dog climbs over Oscar's lap to stare out his window, all the while his tail thumping in my face.

"Get down, you bad boy," Oscar tries to scold him, but Samson pays him no mind. Instead, he starts to whimper and whine in excitement. Apparently, Oscar brings him every year, so he might recognize where we are. Some dogs are that clever.

It's ridiculous, but having him here makes me feel a little braver. Like I've got a friend who will love me no matter what. I pat his bum and he finally sits down between us, so I pet his head.

"Good boy," I murmur, taking deep breaths and doing my best to center my calm. All I have to do is be myself, and Oscar says that's good enough. He's been in this business almost as long as I've been alive. I need to trust his judgment.

Two guys in suits open our doors. "Welcome to Honeyrock!" a beautiful redhead says with a slight accent I think might be Dutch. She smiles brightly as we climb out from the car, then glances at the tablet in her hands. "It's wonderful to see you again, Mr. Wainwright. And is this your guest?"

"Malyk Defries," he says smoothly. It's silly how thrilled I am that he pronounces it perfectly.

Before he can grab both cases again, I wrap my hand firmly around the handle of mine. It was a flattering display of chivalry at the airport, but now that we're here, I don't want to arrive looking like I'm hiding behind him. If I'm going to do this right, I have to stand on my own two feet.

He notices, but then he just smiles and winks before taking his own bag and leading the way up the stairs that take us to the enormous front door.

This house is crazy. It almost *does* look like a castle from a fairy tale. There aren't any turrets, but there are several chimneys. The walls are made from large gray stones, and the windows and balconies are formed of wooden beams. It's huge and looks like it could easily host a medieval king.

It's hosting little ol' me instead, and I resist the urge to giggle.

Rather than head inside, we follow a path around the house that's covered in rose petals and is lined with pillar candles in hurricane jars. I pick my case up so it doesn't disturb the petals too much, then feel a strange little jolt in my heart when I see that Oscar has done the same thing. I like that he's thoughtful, and it reminds me again that with him, I'm in good hands. The hum of conversation gets closer as we near the back of the house, and I try my best not to show my nerves.

That goes out the window when a fucking *shotgun* goes off.

To be fair, I did just about register a woman's voice bellowing *"Pull"* a second before, but I still jump out of my skin and into Oscar's arms.

Yup. In my fear, I leap right into his embrace. Kill me now.

"Sorry, sorry," I splutter as I untangle myself from him and hastily pick up my suitcase from where it slammed to the ground. Luckily, neither it nor I knocked any of the candles over, but I've scattered a fair number of petals out of place.

"Hey, it's fine," says Oscar with a chuckle. Samson is dancing around us, barking, clearly rattled as well. "That scared the bejesus out of me too. Are you okay?"

He reaches out and touches my face, and I'm so stunned that I just stand there and let it happen. Which is probably a good thing in hindsight, as at that moment, someone comes striding around the corner, and we *are* supposed to be a couple, after all. What better way to introduce ourselves than with such an intimate gesture?

Other than my poor heart wanting to beat clean out of my chest, everything's peachy.

"Oscar? Is that you?" the woman asks, cutting

through my brain fog. I blink and see her marching toward us. Then I do a double take.

It's Emmalina.

She has a wild mass of distinctive dark curls and lips painted a glossy blood red. A cape billows around her shoulders, and her knee-high boots have heels that look like they could easily kill a man. Her trousers and waistcoat are tweed. In one hand, she holds the aforementioned shotgun. In the other, a saucer of Champagne.

"Linny!" Oscar cries in relief. "You gave us a fright."

Emmalina waves behind her to indicate the two topless, oiled-up hotties who are following in her wake. One has a strange contraption in his hands, the other the bottle of Champagne.

"Oh, you know I don't like standing still," she says with a scoff, handing the Champagne glass to the guy with the bottle. *"PULL!"*

Immediately, the guy with the contraption points it upward, and a clay disk comes flying out. Emmalina already has her weapon aimed and lets off another shot, this one even louder than before. This time I manage not to hurl myself against Oscar, but I still gasp and slap my hands over my ears as the disk explodes.

"Nice shot," I exclaim in genuine appreciation as I lower my arms, then freeze. Should I have said anything to her? Oscar hasn't even introduced us yet!

But she snorts, glass already back in hand as she takes a swig of Champagne, resting the butt of her gun on her hip. "Thanks, doll. You must be Oscar's new bit of yum." She looks me up and down, then turns to Oscar. "Damn, baby. He's a certified cutie."

"Wait till you see him on film," he says warmly, leaning in to kiss Emmalina on her cheek. "How you been, beautiful?"

"Busy," she says with a dramatic eye roll. "This week couldn't have come fast enough. So let's have some god damned fun, right? Lu, baby?" She takes the Champagne bottle from the guy and blows him an air kiss. "Show my darling Oscar and his friend to his usual room. And you." She spins and clicks a finger in my direction. "Put on something sexy, kitten. Then come back down and tell Auntie Linny all about yourself."

"Okay," I manage not to stammer. I even manage not to spit out that there's nothing interesting about me to tell.

The fact that I'm here is interesting enough.

The shiny fittie in leather pants doesn't say anything. He just nods at Emmalina, then turns and begins to walk toward the house. I grab my case so I'm not left behind, and walk along with Oscar and Samson.

The inside of the almost castle is just as bonkers as the outside. We head in through a side door that leads us down what feels like a workman's entrance, then arrive in a marbled entrance hall. A glittering gold chandelier hangs above us that's as wide as I am tall. Black busts with the tops of their heads missing stand atop plinths all over the place.

"That's the hall of fame," Oscar whispers to me. "Linny's favorite models over the years."

Now that I know what I'm looking at, I think I might even recognize a couple of them.

"Whoa," I say in awe.

Although the majority of guests seem to be outside on the terrace, there are a few people milling around inside as we take the sweeping staircase up. Enough that I can get a sense of what others are wearing. It might only be mid-afternoon, but the vibe seems to be elegant evening wear.

My mind starts whirling as to what I can change into. I might have already met Emmalina, but now she wants to *talk* talk with me, and I want to look like I belong here in her house. I'll also be making my grand entrance to the party proper, and am keen to make a splash. So what if most of my stuff is cheap or thrifted? They don't need to know that. Especially if I wear the shit out of it. Attitude is everything, *dah*-ling.

I'm so busy mentally putting clothes and accessories together that I don't realize we've stopped walking until I bump into Oscar. Heat rushes up my neck and face in embarrassment.

"Sorry," I mumble.

I have *got* to stop throwing myself at this man!

He just winks, though, then turns as our guide opens the door. "Here you are, sir," the topless guy says, handing over an antique-looking key to Oscar. "Enjoy your stay at Honeyrock."

He gives a little bow before striding off, presumably going back to dote on Emmalina. Lucky her.

I'm grinning at my saucy thoughts as I walk into the room Oscar and I will be sharing for the next week, and

I don't immediately understand why Oscar has stopped again. His mood has definitely shifted, though, and I look around the room to work out why.

It doesn't take long.

There's only one bed.

9

OSCAR

I pause for a second before knocking on the door so Malyk can let me back in. I'd chased after Lu—the guy who'd walked us up here—but to no avail.

I should have realized when Emmalina had said it was my usual room. Why didn't it occur to me that there would only be one bed?

Did part of me *want* this to happen?

I shake myself and knock. Of course I didn't. I'd never take advantage of Malyk. *Never.*

His eyebrows are raised as he opens the door for me. "Any joy?" he asks in his lilting accent.

I feel guilty, even though technically it's not my fault. "No, sorry," I say, shaking my head and closing the door behind me.

"You didn't find Mr. Topless?"

I laugh ruefully. Even when we're stressed, he still makes me laugh.

"No, I found him. I also explained that I'd made it clear to Emmalina that I'd requested a room with two beds, which she said would be fine." I roll my eyes. "According to Lu, she thought I was being shy, so let me think that was the case, but there *aren't* any double rooms. And there aren't any free rooms if we wanted our own bed each, so…"

I let my words drift off and glance at the offending bed. It feels like it's radiating heat, even though I'm on the other side of the room still.

Malyk lets out a laugh that's a little too loud to be natural. "Oh, it's *fine*. I mean—look at it. It's ginormous. I bet we could each sleep on either side and still need cups attached by string to chat."

I sigh and rub the back of my neck. "No, it's fine. I'll take the sofa," I say, jutting my chin toward the couch underneath the windowsill. It doesn't look super comfortable—like it's meant more for decoration than actually sitting on—but it's got to be better than the floor, so in that moment I'm grateful for it.

"Oh, no—you don't have to do that!" Malyk cries in distress. "Look—Samson's already on the bed. He's claimed it for you."

I glance over as my dog wags his tail at me like everything's normal, and I can't help but chuckle a little at the ridiculousness of it all. "Honestly, it's fine," I assure him. "This is an incredibly important week for you. You'll need your rest."

And there's *no* way I'm going to risk sleeping in the same bed. Even one so big it practically has two different time zones. Malyk deserves better than that. He demands my respect, and that's what he'll get.

He opens his mouth, no doubt to protest, so I step

forward and wrap my hand around his arm. I know it's playing dirty, but I noticed earlier he listened *very hard* to me when he was in my arms. Immediately, he pauses before he can utter a syllable, and his grayish-green eyes go wide.

"What are you going to wear?" I ask, hoping to distract him.

It works.

"Oh, um," he says, spinning away from me and grabbing his suitcase.

He hauls it up onto the bed by my dog and unzips it with a flourish, splitting it in half so he can inspect the contents. Sam moves his head and gives his tail a halfhearted wag as he sniffs the edge, checking whether or not it's of interest to him.

"I had an idea," he starts explaining. "I'm not sure if it's quite right, though. I'm worried it could be both too fancy and not fancy enough, you know?"

I smile but manage not to laugh. I might spend my working hours capturing beautiful people on film, but ninety-nine percent of the time, you'll find me in good old American denim with a T-shirt or button-down. Clothes aren't a big deal to me.

"I'm sure you'll look stunning in whatever you pick," I assure him. "But why don't you try it on, and I'll give a final verdict?"

He lets out a little sigh of relief and nods. Then he reaches into the case and pulls out a pair of pumps. The chunky heel and platform base are cork, and the straps are denim with beads and feathers attached to them. They look kind of African, and I wonder not for the first time what his heritage is. It hasn't come up, and I believe those kinds of questions are rude to ask unprompted.

"Do you see what I mean?" he says, then chews his lip. "It's kind of fancy but also casual."

I shrug and look outside. "Daytime chic?" I suggest.

He nods thoughtfully. "Plus…I'll be a fucking giant. Would that…um…bother you?"

I frown. "Why would it bother me?"

He's the one to shrug now. "Some guys don't like their date being taller than them. I know we're only pretending, but…"

I scoff. "Sweetie," I say, using the moniker affectionately and genuinely. "I couldn't give a shit. Tower over the mere mortals like the goddess you are."

That gets me a real smile, and I think I've finally gotten through to him.

He sets about picking out the rest of his clothes before heading into the bathroom with a toiletry bag. I take the opportunity to spritz myself with a little after-shave and give Samson a snack to tide him over until dinner. Realistically, I know everyone will slip him tidbits and he'll scarf them all down, because he's part Labrador, and they have bottomless pits for stomachs. But at least I know my chew stick is kind of nutritious and good for his teeth.

I catch up on some emails on my phone while I wait. He calls out once through the door, apologizing for taking so long, but I tell him firmly that the party isn't going anywhere and only losers arrive on time. He laughs and seems to calm down after that.

I'm not sure what I'm imagining him in when he finally emerges, but my jaw drops no matter how prepared I thought I was.

"Fuck me," I say without thinking. Oops.

He blushes and gives me a twirl. I expect a quip or something flirty, but instead he just asks shyly, "Do you like it?"

I swallow. It's not like I haven't seen a million impressive garments in my line of work. It's not the clothes—although those are very nice. No.

It's *him.*

In a way, it's all quite simple. The blue jeans cling to his slender hips and thighs, flaring out slightly around his ankles to highlight the platform heels he showed me first. He's gone for a belt so fine it's practically a necklace that adds just a little sparkle. On the top half, he's tied a sarong of delicate cream fabric at the back of his neck and crossed it over his front so it covers his nipples. The rest flows down almost to the floor. He's finished the look with a beaded necklace that's got a huge pendant that sits just below where the sarong crosses. It's circular and has beads and feathers very similar to the shoes but not exactly matching. His lips, eyelids, and cheekbones show a subtle hint of shimmer.

I'd half-joked about him being a goddess, but that's exactly what he looks like in this moment.

I shake my head and rub the scruff on my chin. "No, Malyk," I say, finally answering his question. "I don't like it. I love it. You look stunning."

I'm pretty sure he could wear a trash bag and he'd still stop traffic. But in this, he's absolutely going to turn heads at a party already filled with very beautiful people.

"Thank you, Oscar," he says, sounding genuinely pleased. Like my opinion matters to him.

"I've been using him," I blurt out in a panic.

Slowly, he blinks at me.

"Using who?" he asks carefully.

Now it's my turn to blush with embarrassment as I wave my hands. "No, I mean you. No! I *mean…*" I take a breath and very quickly reconnect my mouth to my brain. "I mean, I've been using he/him pronouns. Is that correct? I realized I never checked, and I probably should have."

He visibly relaxes, and therefore, so do I. "Oh," he says happily. "That's so nice of you. Um, well, he/him is totally fine. In fact, that's probably safest. I'm not keen on they/them personally but I'll use she/her for myself when I feel like it. But…there are no—like—rules for that and people have used it nastily against me. So, yeah, probs best to avoid. He/him is fine."

His smile is vulnerable, and I can't stop myself from going to him and squeezing his arm. "Of course, sweetheart," I say earnestly. "Is it okay to tell you that you're beautiful?"

He swallows. "It is," he confirms.

For a second, we stare at one another, the tension stretching between us. I can hear my pulse thumping in my ears, and my mouth goes dry. What am I doing? What's happening?

He leans in, just a fraction.

I clear my throat and let out an awkward laugh as I

let go of him and step away. I'm supposed to be looking after him, not confusing him by calling him beautiful and touching his skin or any other irresponsible things like that.

"We should head downstairs," I say with a nod. "Linny's probably eager to meet you."

He also nods and rubs the back of his neck. "Yeah, of course. It's crazy to think she even knows who I am."

"She does, and so will a lot more people before long," I assure him.

It's so much safer to slip back into the mentor role. Maybe not *easier,* but safer.

I turn and look at Samson, who immediately lifts his head and ears in anticipation. "Shall we go out and see our friends?" I ask him.

Malyk and I both laugh as he launches himself off the bed and runs to the door, barking.

"All right, shush now," I admonish him. But the grin on my face probably negates any authority I supposedly have.

Once we make sure we have everything we need, I lock the door and turn back to Malyk, who's now a couple of inches taller than me. I think about what he said about guys not liking him being towering over them. Some men feel that way about women as well. I think that's ridiculous. If you're that insecure about yourself and can't support your date or partner feeling and looking their best, then you probably shouldn't be in a relationship.

In fact, looking up at Malyk stirs something within me that I'd prefer not to examine too closely.

Instead, I offer out my arm for him to hold. "Shall we?"

He bites his glossy lip and nods as he slips his hand over my elbow, and I walk him down the hall. As we approach the stairway, he pauses and raises his eyebrows before looking at me.

"I don't suppose you'd do a quick bit of filming for me—for the Gram?"

"The Gram?" I repeat.

He laughs. "Instagram, Boomer."

"Hey, I'll have you know I'm Gen X," I say huffily. "In fact, I think I just about qualify as a Millennial, depending on who you ask."

He rolls his eyes, but his grin is affectionate as he removes his phone from the small purse he has hanging from his shoulder on a thin strap. Even the bag matches his shoes and jewelry in color and material. His attention to detail won't go unnoticed by this crowd, I'm certain.

"You're lucky I didn't call you 'grampa,'" he teases. "Can you film me walking down the stairs?"

Considering I'm a goddamn photographer for a living, I'm not sure why I take his phone like it's a bomb about to go off. This isn't my medium, I suppose. But film and photo aren't that different. I still know how to frame a shot.

I think it's knowing that he's trusting me with his social media content that's throwing me. Which is stupid. All I have to do is point and film, and he'll decide in a couple of weeks whether it's good enough to upload.

But yet I'm still acting like a teenager hoping to impress the guy I like.

What an idiot.

As it turns out, Malyk does most of the hard work, which is unsurprising, really. He's so easy to capture on camera, and he knows just how to move his body as he struts and poses down the steps. People wordlessly stop for him, not wanting to interrupt the process. The whole thing takes less than five minutes, but the footage we get is flawless.

As I hand back his phone, I realize that doing that little shoot has given me a buzz I haven't felt in years. It was something new and different. Or maybe it was just having him as my subject. Either way, I'm starting to feel less jaded about fashion again. Perhaps I won't be throwing in the towel after all?

When we emerge downstairs into the party proper, I definitely notice a slight stalling in the hum of conversation. Heads absolutely turn, even if it's only for a moment before looking away again so as not to seem too interested. But people want to know who the newcomer is, that much is clear.

Malyk clings to my arm, but his smile is bright as we step out onto the patio together. Emmalina has an irregularly shaped pool sunk into the lawn with a hot tub at the end that people are congregated around. Lights that look like lotus flowers float on the surface, bobbing in the gentle afternoon breeze.

In true Linny style, there is also a small flock of real live flamingos strutting around on the grass, as well as a game of croquet going on by the ice sculpture trickling tequila into waiting glasses. I spot a couple of official-looking guys hanging around to make sure that nobody gets confused with Alice in Wonderland and introduces the birds to the balls.

"Wait till Jamie sees this," Malyk says, shaking his head as he takes a quick couple of photos.

"I thought you weren't posting anything online yet?" I ask. "I mean, you *can*. The event isn't a secret."

"Oh, no," he says shyly. "He's a friend I made—we were sitting together on the fountain when you and I met, remember?"

I do recall the sweet younger boy who had held Malyk's hand when all that shit with Oakley went down. He hadn't even known how to pronounce Malyk's name correctly that day, so it warms my heart that they've obviously stayed in touch. Malyk hasn't really talked about many friends, if any. Just people he knows through work. He deserves good people in his life, though.

Rather than wait staff, Emmalina has several of her regular models serving drinks and light entrées. I say hello to one of the young women I've worked with before and take a couple of Champagne saucers from her, handing Malyk a tall glass of bubbles.

"Ta," he says, taking a sip and looking nervously around. There's a DJ playing music, but it's not so loud that conversations have to be shouted. Samson has already bound off to make new friends and is currently delighting an older lady dressed entirely in black with a dramatic net veil half covering her face and red claws for fingernails.

"Come on," I say, placing my hand on his lower back. "Let's go mingle."

After I introduce him to a couple of acquaintances, he visibly starts to relax, laughing and chatting and just being his fabulous self. I catch one agent giving him an unimpressed look, but he always was a bit of a jealous bitch, so I just take that as a positive sign that Malyk must be doing something right.

When our drinks run out, I volunteer to fetch us fresh glasses, giving Malyk the opportunity to shine on his own. Unfortunately, on my way back to him, I'm waylaid.

"Oscar, you made it," Oakley says, clapping me so hard on the shoulder that the Champagne almost sloshes out of the saucers. "Great to see you again."

I hum and give him a polite smile. It's clear from the two glasses that I'm obviously heading toward someone, but he doesn't seem to care. He just sips on his own drink and looks at me over his sunglasses.

"I just wanted to check everything was okay," he says in concern.

I can't help but frown. "Uh, yeah, sure. Everything's fine." I don't know what he's talking about, and I don't ask for clarification. He keeps talking anyway, and I'm not surprised where the conversation goes.

"Well, just be careful," he says, jutting his chin toward Malyk. He's obliviously talking to another photographer, waving his hands around as she beams at him.

Oakley's words immediately get my hackles up. "What does that mean?" I ask with a tired sigh.

He gives me a one-armed shrug as he sips his drink again. "Just that. Be careful. I know he's pretty, but his goal was obviously to snag an invitation to Honeyrock. He thought he'd convinced me to sneak him in, and then when that failed, he latched onto you. I wouldn't be surprised if you catch him with someone else before the night's through. He's only interested in getting ahead, and he'll fake it with anyone who can help him —especially in bed."

I have to relax my grip on the Champagne so I don't snap the glass stems. How *dare* he say that when he was the one who cheated on Malyk and humiliated him in the middle of a shoot. My smile is even more strained as I nod at him.

"Thanks, but I'm not worried."

He claps my shoulder again and winks. "So long as you look after yourself, mate. I'll see you around, yeah? I need to go find my date and make sure everyone's seen how gorgeous he is." He laughs and saunters off, leaving me with my simmering rage.

He can rewrite the narrative all he wants. He's still very much the asshole in this situation.

I weave my way back to Malyk, some of my anger dissipating when he gives me a warm and genuine smile. "Thanks, babe," he says flirtatiously as I hand him his drink.

I glance subtly behind me. Sure enough, Oakley is staring daggers at us. So I slip my arm around Malyk's waist and tilt my head up to whisper against his ear.

"Do you trust me?" I murmur.

He looks at me with a tiny frown, but he nods. "Of course."

My heart flutters. Even if I'm just protecting him as a friend, I want that trust from him. Especially when what I'm about to do will absolutely cross the line of friendship.

"We're being watched," I say even quieter, like I'm just whispering sweet nothings into my beautiful boyfriend's ear. I jerk my head in Oakley's direction so Malyk knows exactly what I mean. "He thinks you're using me and faking it. Let's show him how real we can be."

His eyes are wide as I pull away to look at him. With my arm still around his waist, our bodies are pressed together, and I can feel his heart thumping in his chest. I lean in, giving him a chance to back off if he doesn't consent. But he stays exactly where he is, his lips parted and inviting.

It's just for show, I remind myself. *We're just proving that prick Oakley wrong.*

My heart doesn't get the memo, though, as I finally press my mouth to Malyk's, kissing the absolute hell out of him.

10

MALYK

Oh my god.

Oh my fucking god.

We'd talked about doing some PDA, but we'd agreed on holding hands and maybe the odd peck on the cheek. But Oscar Wainwright is one hundred percent snogging my face off right now.

ARGH!

I cling to his shoulder, and his fingers dig into my back as the kiss deepens. His tongue dances with mine and his lips claim my own with a fierce possession I wouldn't have thought he was capable of. He tastes of sweet Champagne and a delicious saltiness, I guess from the food, and his woodsy aftershave engulfs me.

I almost want to thank Chris for being such a wanker. This is *amazing*.

Far too soon, though, he pulls away from me, panting. His eyes are wide, and he looks as stunned as I feel. Yeah, there was *nothing* fake about that bad boy. Neither is the thickening of my cock in my jeans. *Fuck.* I wonder if he's getting hard as well.

He clears his throat and steps away from me so I don't find out. "I think that did the trick," he says with a chuckle, glancing over to where I assume Chris is or was watching us. I don't even look. I couldn't give a shit about that prick in this moment.

I only have eyes for Oscar.

"Uh, yeah," I say hoarsely, hardly remembering what he just said. Oh, yeah. Fooling Chris. "That'll learn him."

"Darling!" a familiar voice cries over the thrum of the party. "There you are!"

I'm jolted from my lusty thoughts by realizing that Emmalina is cutting through the crowd and making a beeline for me. Samson is trotting by her feet, looking thrilled, and I wonder if he led our host over to us.

"Linny," Oscar says warmly, the weird spell between us broken. But he still keeps his hand on my back as he kisses her cheek, and I can't help but revel in the touch. It's getting harder and harder to remember why I made myself promise not to get involved with anyone in the industry again.

Oscar feels different. *So* different.

"Aren't you a vision?" Emmalina coos at me.

"Nothing compared to you," I manage to say without stumbling over my words.

It's true, however. I wasn't the only one to nip inside for a costume change. She's ditched the fancy hunting look for an elegant, sparkly halter neck dress in midnight blue. Her gold Grecian sandals give it a slightly more casual air than high heels would have, but the twenty bangles on each wrist clatter when she moves her arms, and they don't sound like imitation metal at all.

She laughs and tosses her voluminous hair over her shoulder. "What, this old thing?" she drawls, giving me a slow spin. It's backless down to her hips, showing off her lower back where there's a tattoo of roses and skulls that her brand is so well known for. "It's got to be—what? At least two seasons old. Practically ancient."

I almost feel a wave of insecurity. My jeans weren't cheap, but they're still only from the high street. However, then she winks at me and clinks our glasses together like she's letting me in on a secret, and I relax a fraction. She's not judging me on my clothes, after all. She's judging me on my ability to sell *her* clothes.

"So, Oscar," she says mischievously. "Where have you been hiding this diamond?"

"We only met a couple of weeks ago," he says, squeezing my hip.

My heart flutters, and I lick my lips nervously. I can still taste him, and it only makes me want more. If I wasn't talking to one of the most important designers in America, I would have had trouble concentrating. But I manage to keep my brain focused and not let my thirsty cock take over.

I have no idea what will happen between me and Oscar once this conversation is over, but for now, thoughts of being on the cusp of a massive career opportunity help me behave. This is my chance to genuinely make a name for myself and stand on my own two feet.

"Yeah, it's been a whirlwind romance," I say shyly. That's *almost* true.

She flicks her eyebrows suggestively. "Naughty boys. I *was* talking about your beautiful face, though. You're signed, yes?"

"Oh, yeah. Yes," I amend, trying not to be so casual. "I'm with McKay Models—the London branch. They found me through my Instagram."

She clicks her fingers several times. "Show me, show me!" she says excitedly, beckoning for my phone.

I can't deny that I'm nervous as I hand it over, but it's not all bad. I'm very proud of my Insta and keep it extremely well maintained. But that won't necessarily mean she'll like my work. I just have to trust that if she wants a peek into my portfolio, I know I've given myself the best chance I can with all that past effort.

Her eyebrows shoot up as soon as she starts scrolling through my account. I have a mixture of photos and videos, and I just watch her quietly as she skims through them, giving her time to assess.

"Damn, darling," she says eventually, shaking her head. "This is impressive. And you've worked with Oscar as well?"

"We did a campaign last week," I say, feeling coy as she returns my phone. "It was amazing."

"I'll send you some of the early mockups from the campaign once I get them," Oscar tells her with a wink. "It was a very special day."

"And I heard the person who facilitated it is a

genius," an unfortunately familiar voice drawls far too close to my ear for my liking. I can't help but whip my head around and scowl at Chris. After a second, I compose myself and school my features, but he's already laughing. "Only joking," he quips. "Although it was a great day. Everyone should be proud of their work."

I hum noncommittally with a nod, then glance at the pretty guy beside him. Chris is slightly turned away, giving all of his attention to Oscar and Emmalina, but the petite blond man by his elbow is clearly with him by his hopeful expression.

I feel a slight pang of rejection before I remember that I'd rather be here with Oscar than Chris any day of the week. If this is his new fling or boyfriend or what-ever, I say good luck to him. Chris obviously doesn't care enough about him to introduce him.

So I do it for him.

"Hi, I'm Malyk," I say, thrusting my hand out toward him and thereby forcing him into our little circle of conversation.

He looks at me with immense relief and suddenly seems a lot younger. I question how old he actually is. "Hi, I'm Frans," he says with a slight accent I can't place but assume is some kind of European. He shakes my hand with a delicate grip. "I love your shoes."

I kick out my heel a little and preen. "Thanks, gorge. I love your shirt."

It's black gauze with colorful roses embroidered onto it, and it clings nicely to his slim torso. There's no denying that he's beautiful, but I wonder if allying himself with Chris will get him as far as he hopes.

"Frans is a fresh face on the scene," Chris says smugly, getting his phone out. "If we're looking at Instagram, then his is—"

"Oh, yes, *wonderful,* dear," Emmalina interrupts, patting him on the cheek. "I'd absolutely love to take a peek, but I appear to be out of Champagne, and that simply won't do." She drains the last of her saucer, then saunters off with a wink in my direction.

I definitely feel bad for Frans. If there's a way to help him out later, I'll certainly try. But I can't help but feel gleeful that our eminent host snubbed my grotty ex so obviously. Serves him right for trying to hijack our conversation.

"Are you with an agency?" Oscar asks Frans politely.

The younger guy beams at him. "Not yet, but Chris said he'd help me. He found me through my Instagram."

"Me, too," I say with a light touch on his shoulder like it's the cutest coincidence in the world. I hate that I owe my signing at McKay's to Chris, and that he still has so much power over my career as my agent, but maybe things will turn out better for Frans.

Or maybe Chris is just using him this week to try and teach me some sort of lesson. Who knows? I hope that whatever happens, this sweet guy doesn't get a raw deal.

Oscar asks to see some of Frans' work. As the younger model unlocks his phone and starts chatting to my date, Chris uses the opportunity to lean in and murmur to me.

"I don't know what game you're playing, but it won't

last," he says in a pleasant tone with a smile that doesn't reach his eyes.

I look him up and down. "I'm not playing any games," I say coolly, my voice not as quiet as his. I only feel a little guilty for lying. But what Oscar and I are doing isn't really a game. Sure, the fake-dating part is, maybe. And that kiss we just shared might say other-wise, but we only decided to run along with that little white lie because Chris put us in that position.

My invitation here and Oscar's friendship is genuine.

Samson suddenly barks. I'd quite forgotten he was there. He's been wandering around getting attention from people nearby, but apparently, now he's done with this particular conversation and is letting us know about it.

Oscar laughs and pets his head. "Oh, is it dinner time? Thank you for reminding me, greedy guts," he says fondly. Then he nods at Chris and Frans. "Excuse me, but I need to deal with my demanding dog."

"I'll come with you," I say quickly, not wanting to be left alone with my ex and his new bit of stuff.

What I don't realize is that will leave me alone with *Oscar* as we pop back up to the room. My heart is thumping in my chest, but Oscar seems perfectly calm as he leads us back upstairs and lets us through the door. Like that kiss didn't completely rock his world.

Bollocks. That puts cold water on a lot of my hopes and fantasies.

"That Chris Oakley is a peach," he says with a scoff as he quickly gets Samson a bowl of meaty dinner.

I roll my eyes and hug my Champagne glass to my chest. "Yeah, he's a charmer," I say, my words dripping with sarcasm. Quite frankly, I'm grateful to talk about something that isn't us if he's not going to address the kiss. "Did he actually warn you off me?"

"He said you were using me," Oscar says with a laugh. "I think it's pretty clear to anyone paying attention who's the fake one down there."

I chew my lip. I want to ask him *not* to fake it, then. To be with me, for real, even if it's just for this week. But I'm afraid he'll reject me. He's made it clear that he doesn't date models and that I'm too young. He's just doing me a favor. So I laugh nervously instead and shrug.

"He told me to stop playing games as well. Like he hasn't brought that pretty boy here just to start drama."

Oscar moves closer to me and squeezes my arm. *Fuck.* He keeps doing that and every time I want to melt.

"Don't worry," he assures me. "Emmalina saw right through all that. You, though." He lets go and wags a finger at me. "You she was impressed with."

I swallow, hardly daring to believe it. "Really?"

"Oh, yeah," he says with a nod. "That doesn't mean anything's guaranteed. But you keep being your fabulous self for the next few days, and there's a strong chance she'll want you involved with the winter range. Maybe even Paris Fashion Week."

That really does make me feel sick. Runway modeling is my dream, but the idea of walking one of the most prestigious shows on the planet absolutely seems too good to be true.

Speaking of 'too good to be true,' Oscar moves even farther away from me toward the door, reminding me that the kiss we shared really was just for show. He's not about to repeat it now that we have some privacy.

I'll be replaying it over and over again, though. In fact, it's all I can do for the rest of the party to pay attention to whoever's talking to me. I give it my all as I network and socialize, but in the back of my mind lingers the way his fingers felt digging into my skin and the taste of his lips on mine.

As I lay in bed hours later, I feel even worse, knowing that he's sleeping mere feet away from me. So close yet so far. I yearn to touch myself as I fantasize about his mouth on mine, but until I can snatch a moment alone, I press my fingertips to my lips instead, smiling in the darkness.

That kiss might have been a performance, but that doesn't mean it wasn't real to *me*.

11

—————

OSCAR

I might grumble about getting old, but I know I'm not *actually* old.

Unfortunately, my back when I wake up doesn't seem to have gotten the memo.

I give my neck a good crack and figure that and a hot shower will fix the throbbing ache between my shoulder blades, but sadly, whatever I've pulled is still twinging like a mother fucker every time I twist the wrong way or reach out with my arms at the wrong angle.

Shit. This is not ideal.

I pop some anti-inflammatory painkillers and decide to go on the hunt for a tennis ball. There's bound to be one around here. I just have to look. If I roll that between my back and a wall real good, hopefully, that might work out some kinks. I also have a plan to grab a spot in the hot tub that's situated at the end of Linny's pool.

By the time I'm dressed and ready to head out,

Malyk is still dead asleep. I'm not surprised. We did drink a fair bit last night and were up pretty late. I find my notebook and rip out a page so I can leave him a message letting him know I've gone for a walk. As I place it on his nightstand along with a fresh glass of water for him to find when he awakes, I have a mad urge to lean down and kiss his cheek.

That would be so wrong.

Yet I pause for a good ten seconds, debating with myself before Samson's headbutt to my leg brings me to my senses.

Yeah. *Seriously* wrong.

I jerk my head silently at my dog, figuring he's probably going to want to stretch his legs. I love that he understands that this is quiet time and doesn't bark as we head out of the door. I'd hate it if he'd woken up Malyk when he's sleeping so peacefully.

I curse that ornate couch more than once as we walk around Emmalina's grounds. It feels like I've nudged a damn rib out of place or something. I'm going to have to work on my poker face, though. I'm not spoiling Malyk's day with my complaining.

Especially not when he shone like a star last night.

He didn't just dazzle Linny. He impressed everyone he met, I could tell. Well, expect for Oakley, but he doesn't count. Oakley's *date* was even charmed by Malyk's genuine nature, quick wit, and stunning beauty. Anyway, Malyk doesn't need to impress his ex. The man is *supposed* to be Malyk's agent, the person advocating for him and helping him succeed in this perilous industry. Except he's more like the shark swimming silently below the surface of the water, waiting to savage any toe Malyk tries to dip in the water.

I grit my teeth and pause on our walk around the wooded grounds of Emmalina's place. Samson looks up at me, his tail wagging. It's not like me to get this worked up over anything. But the idea of someone hurting Malyk just makes me crazy.

And—if I'm being truly honest with myself—if I'm getting mad over Oakley, that means I'm not thinking about that kiss.

That fucking kiss.

Dear sweet baby Jesus.

How could Oakley cheat on someone so gorgeous? The sexual energy just drips off the man, for crying out loud. It seems completely impossible that he'd be disappointing in bed.

I rub my forehead and sigh, knowing I'm safe and no one can hear me. I really shouldn't be thinking of him like that, but it's becoming impossible not to.

I finish my walk with Samson and manage to find a tennis ball in the game room downstairs. The house and grounds are still reasonably quiet—it seems most people are sleeping in after last night's festivities. The first and last days are always the biggest parties, so I'm not surprised. The privacy gives me a few minutes to work the ball between my shoulder blades against a wall. It takes the edge off, but I'm not convinced that it really fixed anything.

Oh well. It's not like I'm planning to go rock climbing or whatever. In fact, today I'm very much looking forward to lounging around by the pool. It's been a while since I took a vacation. I always have to remind myself that traveling for work doesn't count. I just need to lie in the sun with a cocktail and float in the pool, all the while trying to keep my thoughts PG-13.

Hmm. Maybe that won't be as relaxing as I hope.

Especially when I get back to the room to find Malyk looking at himself in the mirror, wearing nothing but a tiny pair of leopard print swim briefs. I'm not sure what's worse, the way they hug his tight ass and substantial cock, or all the delicious skin they leave on display.

"Oh, sorry," he says with a little laugh and quickly grabs a gauzy robe to throw over himself. "You said today was going to be a pool party, so I wanted to pick my best outfit."

Technically, every day will be a pool party, but rather than correct him it's all I can do to nod and move over to my own drawers.

I'm suddenly not sure about the shorts I've got to wear. I think I've got a pretty decent body—I work out at the gym regularly enough and like running—but he's just otherworldly. It's very unlike me to be insecure. However, I have an irrational fear that he's going to laugh at me. Because I could be as fit as possible, but that still won't change the fact that I'm eighteen years older than him.

And then I remember who the hell I'm thinking about. Do I really believe Malyk would be a shallow prick and judge me or make me feel bad? No, never. He's far too kind. Besides—do I wish that I was twenty-four like he is? Also no. I was a mess at his age, and I don't think we'd get along at all. So what's there to be worried or ashamed of?

"Are you ready to head down for breakfast?" I ask him as I get the shorts out with a T-shirt as well as a bottle of sunscreen. I think I can cope with this aggravating back pain, but sunburn on top of that would be too much.

"Oh, yeah," he says as he tries on a delicate gold necklace. "I'm starving."

I chuckle at his never-ending appetite. "There's a buffet every morning and one for lunch, too," I inform him as I step into the bathroom to change. "Dinner is usually a mixture of party food like last night or more formal sit-down meals." I stick my head out of the door and wink at him. "Not everyone is invited to those, but we will be."

"Oh," he says softly with a bashful smile. "Thank you."

I retreat back into the bathroom and bite my lower lip, my heart fluttering. The reason I never wanted to ever date a model is because so many of them that I've met have a very unattractive air of entitlement around them. It's unavoidably true that beauty gets you very, very far in life. People treat you differently.

But Malyk isn't like that. He's still acting like he can't believe that he's here, that he's special.

That humility is extremely attractive.

Aaaand there's the damn kiss popping up in my brain again. Honestly, though, who could blame me? It was electrifying. Mind-blowing. And then I walk in to find him practically naked, looking like a frigging marble statue carved by a Renaissance master.

It occurs to me that he did that on purpose. That he *wanted* me to catch him.

Perhaps I need to stop dismissing his flirting as something casual he'd do with anyone. I'm so worried about getting hurt again like I did with Jerry, but am I in danger of missing out on something incredible? Or worse, of hurting *Malyk?* That's the absolute last thing I want. In fact, we got into this whole situation because I decided frighteningly fast that I'd go to great lengths to protect him.

But that could get messy—so messy. What if we sleep together and it all goes wrong then we're stuck with each other all week?

Or what if we fuck and it's incredible and then after the week is over, we have to go our separate ways? His life is in London. Mine's here in New York.

I'm not sure what scenario stresses me out more.

I can't think on an empty stomach, so I finish getting changed and lotion my legs, arms, and face. I can do the rest if I decide to get in the pool. Mercifully, Malyk is a little more covered up now with denim shorts under the sarong-robe. His sunglasses are huge and stylish. I'd look ridiculous in them, but he's just as glamorous as ever.

"Shall we?" he says saucily, popping a hand on his hip and peering over the large glasses. Samson barks and chases his tail once before looking up happily at me.

"We shall," I say, inclining my head.

There are more people milling around than before,

and I assume they, like us, have been driven out of their beds by their stomachs. My mouth waters as we enter the dining room that's been set up with dozens of plates of fruits, breads and spreads, yogurts, various kinds of milk and cereals, and pastries. And that's not even mentioning the hot station that's crammed with trays of eggs, bacon, waffles, and crispy shredded hash browns. There's also coffee, juices, and even smoothies.

"Praise the lord," Malyk moans, pressing his hands together.

I chuckle and follow him as he sashays toward the stack of plates, pleased to see that he doesn't hesitate to load his up. It took a lot of coaxing to get him to relax and enjoy all the luxuries when we were flying, but he finally seems to be getting the hang of this lifestyle that I'm really hoping he'll be experiencing a lot more of.

My main concern is a vat of coffee. Once I drain my first cup, I can think straight again. I didn't have as much to drink last night as most people, but it was still several glasses. Caffeine and carbs are definitely essential this morning.

By the time I have more food on my plate than is probably strictly necessary, I look around but can't see Malyk anymore. I frown but figure he can't have gone far. Sure enough, once I make my way out to the pool with Samson at my side, I see him lounging on a deck chair in one of the best spots on the patio. He's thrown his robe on the one next to it, and he excitedly pats it when he sees me. My heart flips when I realize he's saved it for me.

Also when I realize that he's only in his swimming briefs again. Hot damn.

"I got us a Bloody Mary each," he announces in delight. I notice as I walk over to him that there are servers carrying trays of the drinks around.

I laugh and grimace. "You might have to let me have breakfast first before I get back on it." He just shrugs and grins, unfazed.

"Sure thing, old man," he says sweetly.

I glower, then snap my fingers at him. "Give it here, brat."

He cackles as he hands it over, fluttering his eyelashes innocently. "It's good for you, I promise."

Damn him and his youth. I'm sure I'll regret it, but I can't deny that I'm grinning as I give the cocktail a sip. I can't remember the last time I felt this joyful or carefree.

I catch Samson trying to sneak some bacon off my plate, and rescue it just in time. But he looks so forlorn as I settle on the sun lounger with my plate that I relent and feed it to him anyway.

"You softie," Malyk says with a warm laugh.

I know I'll have to put my dog on a strict diet next week, but I can't deny it's adorable seeing him so happy. Especially when he realizes he's not getting any more treats from me, so he spins around and gives Malyk a pitiful face instead.

"You liar!" Malyk cries, but he still tosses Samson a bit of potato anyway.

I laugh just the wrong way, and suddenly the dull ache in my back becomes blinding pain. I feel my face screw up as I reach back and grab at it, like that's going to make any difference. But the damage is done. Malyk's expression is horrified.

"What's wrong?" he yelps, abandoning his plate and jumping to sit by my side.

Right next to my side. In nothing but those blasted briefs.

Fuck my life. Even as the pain fades, my cock still has some life in it, as it jumps in my shorts.

"Ah, nothing," I say, trying to play it down. "Just pulled a muscle or something."

Malyk scowls. "I *told* you to sleep on the bed," he hisses. "Show me where it hurts."

"It's fine," I grumble, rolling my shoulders and willing the pain away. Funnily enough, it doesn't work. "I just need to get in the hot tub."

He huffs and takes my plate off me, placing both it and his on the little table between our sun loungers. "No," he says firmly to Samson with a pointed finger. To his credit, my dog lies down and rests his head on his paws, looking up at us with big eyes. "Good boy," Malyk says with a twitch of a smile. Then he turns back to me and stands. "You, on your front."

I lick my lips nervously. "Why?"

He rolls his eyes but also chuckles. "So I can watch you tap dance. Why do you think? I did a short course on massage therapy. Let me see if I can help."

I swallow and try not to panic. I have to be honest that I'd appreciate any help with this pain, but that's going to mean Malyk putting his hands on my body.

"Oh, you don't have to," I say in a pitiful attempt to give him one last chance out.

He tuts and waves his hands. "Come on. Shirt off. I can use suntan lotion instead of oil, and that way you'll have UV protection as well. Win-win."

He grins, clearly pleased with himself. So I sigh and resign myself to my fate. I pull my T-shirt off and get as comfortable as I can with the lounger laid out flat.

He takes a pillow from a nearby chair and kneels beside me. I'm aware there are people around us before I close my eyes, but we're not doing anything wrong, so I try not to worry about them and relax.

This isn't foreplay. It's medical. Malyk is doing me a service.

I describe where the offending area is, and he runs his fingers between my shoulder blades a few times before starting to really knead into my flesh. He seems to actually know what he's doing and is confident as he works my twinging muscles.

But then his hands explore upward, and he scoffs. "You're like a rock," he admonishes. "Enough knots to get a Scout badge. That's it. I'm putting my foot down. You're not sleeping on that couch again."

"It's fine," I protest feebly. But to be honest, my focus is being drawn to a different problem right now that's demanding all of my attention.

I'm getting hard.

I think I can control it or at least conceal it, but then—sweet baby *Jesus*—he climbs on top of me, straddling my ass as he leans his full weight back between my shoulder blades. I let out a groan before I can stop myself, but at this point, I'm not sure how much resistance I have left.

"This is supposed to be uncomfortable," Malyk says, oblivious to the true cause of my suffering. "The massage I mean—not the couch. I could have told you that was a bad idea. In fact, I did. But if anything actually hurts, let me know, okay?"

I clear my throat. "No, no. It's good," I say honestly. "I think it's working."

"Great," he cries cheerfully, then continues to manhandle me.

I grit my teeth and breath steadily in and out of my nose, trying to think of repulsive things in order to calm myself down. But it's pretty much impossible while Malyk is practically riding my ass as he works his elbows, fingers, and the heels of his hands into my sore muscles.

"There we go, that's starting to feel looser," he murmurs. "What do you think?"

I hum and try not to tremble as he runs his hands up and down my sides. "Uh, yeah," I croak. "Good. Better, I think."

He gets off me and kneels back on the cushion, a warm smile on his lips. I turn my head and rest it on my folded arms. He really does look like a gift from the gods. How could anyone's face be so perfect?

"Brilliant," he says. "I'm glad I could help. But I'm serious. You can't sleep on that decorative couch again. I don't like seeing you in pain, and I'm putting my foot down."

He scowls, and I know he's trying to tell me off, but

he's just so adorable and my heart is swelling with deep affection at his genuine concern for me. I'm the one who swore to look after him, and yet here he is coming to my rescue. He cares for me just as much as I care for him.

I lift my head and shoulders to rotate my vision and look at him properly. Our faces are so close together, and I'm aware of my pulse thumping in my ears. My breaths are shallow, and I lick my lips. "Malyk…?" I say faintly.

I don't know what I'm trying to ask. But he holds my gaze and also licks his lips, his chest rising and falling. Then he carefully reaches out and touches my arm.

"Oscar," he says with conviction.

I'm not sure what happens. It's like something breaks inside me. I surge forward and claim his mouth with my own, my heart leaping when he responds immediately, kissing me back with fervor, his hands seizing either side of my face like he's afraid I'll run away. He tastes like sunshine and the tangy, rich cocktail he was just drinking.

This isn't like the kiss we shared for Oakley's benefit. Oh no. Despite all the people around us, this is intimate and fiery. I prop myself up on my elbow and reach out with the other hand to cup the back of his neck. The kiss deepens, and I never want it to stop, but it can't go on forever, as we have to breathe.

He breaks away, gasping for air, his pupils blown and his cheeks flushed.

Just as quickly as something snapped in me before,

it does so again. But if last time was a flame bursting to life, this is a bucket of cold water dousing it.

"*Fuck,*" I rasp, scrambling off the sun lounger. "Malyk, I'm sorry. I…fuck…*sorry.*"

I can't think straight. Horror is crawling through me. I promised to *protect* him, not take *advantage* of him.

Maybe he should have held on to me tighter when he had the chance. Because in that moment, it's all I can do to snatch up my shirt and flee back to the safety of our room.

12

MALYK

For a second, I simply kneel in shock, not sure what the hell just happened. Samson whimpers and brings me back to my senses in time to see Oscar rush back into the house. I swallow and touch my lips.

Did I push things too far?

"Oh no," I utter, then look down at Samson who's wagging his tail anxiously. "I think I over-flirted," I whisper in horror to him.

Yes, Oscar really did need that massage. His back was a mess, and he definitely has to take care of it—namely by sleeping on a proper mattress tonight. But I didn't need to climb on *top* of him like a wanton hussy.

I was just tired of feeling like my intentions weren't coming through clearly enough. But maybe I should have used my *words* instead of my *arse* to convey that.

Hang on, though. *He* kissed *me* just now. And it wasn't like last night, when we'd been putting on a show for Chris. No one had been watching. That was just something between us—two people who couldn't resist the pull between them any longer.

Or at least that's what I felt.

So I should do something about it.

I jump to my feet and slide them back into my flip-flops as I throw the robe over my shoulders and grab my bag. Neither of us hardly touched a bite on our breakfast plates, but food is going to have to wait.

Right now, our hearts are on the line.

Thankfully, just at that moment, Emmalina comes swanning out of the dining room in a sun hat about a meter wide, her signature saucer of Champagne in one hand and a bowl of strawberries in the other. I dash over to her, briefly noting how crazy it is that she's the person I feel most confident asking a favor of right now.

"Emmalina, hi—good morning," I say breathlessly. "Could you possibly keep an eye on Samson? Oscar isn't, um, feeling well, and I need to go find him."

She sighs with deep fondness. "Sure thing, doll. You go look after your man. Little Sammy is all good with Auntie Linny. Tell Oscar I hope he feels better soon."

Her grin is somewhat salacious, and I'm sure she's got something spicier in mind than me cuddling him better. But honestly, I have no idea what to expect. So I just nod at her gratefully, then run off into the house.

I don't see him in the dining room or the lobby and almost start to panic. But then I remember that he doesn't have a car here, so there's only so far he could have gone. I decide to do the obvious thing and check our room first, and if that's no good, I can continue to wander.

One thing's for sure, and that is that I won't stop looking until I find him.

My heart aches as I climb the stairs. Yeah, yeah, I know logically that he was the one who kissed me, but only after I'd been doing some pretty hard-core flirting. He's been so kind and generous to me. I'd absolutely hate it if I'd put him in some kind of uncomfortable situation.

I pause for a second in front of our door and take a couple of deep breaths. If he wants to go back to just being friends, that's okay. I can cope with that.

I won't be okay if he hates me now.

"Oscar?" I say softly as I tap on the door. "Are you there? May I come in?"

It's probably only a few seconds I have to wait, but it feels like forever. But then I hear him clear his throat. "Yeah, come in," he says.

I'm far from being out of the woods, but I can't deny the relief that flows through me with just those few words. Okay, I've found him.

Now what?

Time to find out, I guess.

It's unlocked, so I turn the handle and let myself inside. His T-shirt is back on. He's standing by the foot of the bed, looking out of the window with his arms wrapped around himself. It's both defensive and protective, and I ache for him.

"I'm so sorry," he says before I've even closed the door, shaking his head miserably.

I wait for the click so I know we have some privacy, then drop my bag and slip off my flip-flops before padding over to him, also shaking my head. "You've got *nothing* to be sorry for," I insist. "I'm sorry I pushed things. We had clear rules, and I tried to break them."

He finally meets my gaze with his own and offers me a weak smile. "Are they clear, though, those rules we set up?"

I bite my lip and step a little closer. "Not really," I admit. It all seemed so simple when we came up with this little scheme in that Thai restaurant back in London. Fuck it. Why am I fighting this *so* hard? Oscar isn't Chris. He never could be. "I...I really like you, Oscar. I wanted you to kiss me back there. I was pretty gutted when you bolted."

"Oh, Malyk," he says, sounding heartbroken. He pulls me into a fierce hug and holds me tightly for a few moments. "Hurting you was the *last* thing I wanted to do. I convinced myself if I acted on these feelings, *that* would be what hurt you, but I think I've managed to fuck up anyway." He sighs deeply and digs his fingers into my skin through the robe, making my heart skip a beat. "I really like you, too."

I gently run my hands up and down his back before leaning away so we can see each other when I speak. "Then what are we doing?" I ask. "What are we hiding from?"

He studies me. "I'm supposed to be taking care of you," he protests feebly.

I scoff, but it's not unkind. "You *are,*" I insist. "No one's ever looked after me like you do. I feel..."

This is hard. Chris taught me it was dangerous to be vulnerable and honest. He threw my hopes and dreams back in my face with a laugh. But I know Oscar would never do that to me.

"You make me feel special and cherished and safe. If that's not taking care of me, then I don't know what is."

He nibbles his lip, worry still evident on his features. "We have less than a week left together," he whispers. "What do you want from me?"

I shake my head. "I can't fret about the future," I say earnestly. "No plans I've ever made have worked out like I thought they would. All I can do is live in the now and seize every opportunity I can." I nudge my hip against his and feel a cautiously optimistic smile play on my lips. "That includes you, old man."

He doesn't laugh, though, and I curse myself. "I *am* so much older than you," he protests.

I roll my eyes and stamp my foot. "I don't give a shit," I cry with a frustrated laugh. "Stop making excuses. Unless…" I lose my fight. "If you're not that attracted to me, then I'll back the fuck off and never bring it up again." I let go and step away.

Or at least I try to.

He grabs my hip and yanks me crashing back into him, our chests colliding and our faces stopping only a couple of inches apart.

"I *never* said I wasn't attracted to you, you brat," he growls.

Holy fucking shit. It's a good thing he's got his arms wrapped around me like steel because in that moment I turn to goo. "Is that so?" I say breathlessly. "Are you sure? Aren't I an annoying little whippersnapper? You didn't seem all that impressed when I showed off my teeny bikini bottoms this morning. In fact, you seemed terrified."

He drops his arms and grabs two firm handfuls of my arse. "I fucking *knew* you were teasing me on purpose," he snarls. My heart races like I'm prey caught in a predator's paws.

"Me?" I whisper innocently, fluttering my eyelashes. His mouth is so close to mine that his breath is ghosting over my lips. It's rich with the scent of coffee.

"You," he rasps back.

I hum. "Maybe I *was* waiting for you to come back so I could show off. So what are you going to do about it?"

He spins us and I gasp as I fall backward onto the bed. "This," he says as he crawls over my body.

When he claims my mouth this time, I'm pretty confident he's not going to run away.

I wrap my legs around his waist just to make sure.

13

MALYK

The teasing was worth it. The honesty was worth it. Because now Oscar is kissing the shit out of me and grinding his body on top of mine like he means business.

This is a working holiday, after all. A little business is the order of the day, I'm sure.

His body is twice the size of mine and firm. He smells of coconut from the suntan lotion but also a spicy masculine musk that I want to drink in. I taste the coffee stronger on his mouth as our lips meet over and over and our tongues reach out to explore. Then he's kissing along my jawline, his beard tickling against my skin. I hum in sheer delight and squeeze my legs tighter around him.

"Yes," I hiss, pulling at his T-shirt. I want it off again, now.

He chuckles and pauses his kisses to help me lift it off and throw it onto the floor. I groan and run my hands through his chest hair, loving the coarseness. I'm slim, not particularly muscular, and waxed smooth, but I like the contrast between us. I also really like feeling pinned down by someone rugged and more experienced than I am.

"You're so beautiful," he mumbles as he kisses down my throat. "Inside and out."

I bite my lip and screw my eyes shut as emotion wells up within me. It's not like I haven't been told I'm beautiful before. But when Oscar says it…it's like it's got a completely different meaning to it. I feel it in my soul.

Shivers run all over my body as his fingers trace along the sides of my chest. He rubs his thumbs over my nipples, making them harden into buds. His mouth finds mine again, and I use my legs to haul myself upward and rub my hips against his. There are far too many layers between us, and my cock is begging for release.

"I didn't bring anything with me," I blurt out, meaning condoms and lube. Because apparently, I was in such denial that I didn't fathom the possibility of sex with anyone, let alone Oscar.

He nuzzles our noses together and drags my lower lip between his teeth. "That's all right, gorgeous. Neither did I. But right now, I just want to see you come."

I whimper and kiss his mouth again, hard. "You, too," I insist. Then my eyes fly open, and I loosen my hold on him with all four of my limbs. "Oh my god," I whisper in horror. "Is your back okay?"

He throws his head back and laughs before kissing me sweetly. "It's much better. You have a magic touch."

My concern is immediately replaced by lust. "Oh, I'll show you a magic touch," I threaten, dropping my hands to attack his swimming shorts. Suddenly, I'm very appreciative of the handy elasticated waist.

He grins and helps shove them down, moving his legs and kicking them off the bed with his T-shirt.

And just like that, he's completely naked on top of me.

Hairy thighs blend into an even hairier thatch between his legs where his dick is straining out toward me. It's not super long, but it's got a good girth and curves a little to his right. I wrap my fingers around it, groaning at how hard and hot it is. I rub my thumb over the already leaking tip, loving the way that makes him gasp and bury his face against my neck.

"Can I suck you off?" I ask against the shell of his ear before nipping at the lobe.

He pants and nods. "Fuck, yes," he agrees.

In a flash, he's rolled over onto his back, and I release my hold fully from around his waist. I need my legs back so I can do something about the *two* pairs of shorts I'm still unfairly wearing. First, though, I go to slip the gauzy robe off, but he reaches up suddenly and stops me.

"Keep that on," he says. It's not a request, and I love that. God, I know he's said so many times that I'm beautiful, but I want to be *so* hot for him. I want to blow his mind.

So I nod and bite my lip shyly, agreeing to his command. But the denim shorts are gone in a flash.

Buh-bye. They were only there for modesty purposes anyway, and that's all flown out the window now.

I love the way that the tight and silky material of my swimwear feels against my throbbing, leaking cock, so I keep them on for the time being. Plus, I like the idea of leaving a little something to anticipate, so on they stay.

I don't hear any complaints from Oscar as I crawl back up the bed, gripping tightly onto his thick thighs and nuzzling my nose against the root of his length, tonguing at his heavy balls. His scent is stronger down here in his more intimate areas, and when I lick a stripe up the underside of his length, it's salty and delicious.

He moans and slips his fingers through my hair, watching me through his eyelashes. "Gorgeous," he says reverently.

I feel powerful as I swallow him down halfway, rubbing my tongue over the slitted head, seeing how he bucks and twitches under me. Chris liked to boss me around in bed, which was fine, I guess. But I'm really loving how Oscar is giving himself over to me. His whole energy is just so mellow and chilled.

Although he's not exactly *passive* as he thrusts up into my mouth and tugs at my hair. Good. I'd have hated it if he'd been boring or lazy in bed.

I hum as I pleasure him, perfectly happy to make him come like this and worry about myself later. But he tugs at my hair, encouraging me to pop off and move back up the bed to kiss him. "I want you," he mumbles into my mouth, rubbing my cock through the silky swimwear.

"You've got me," I assure him.

But he shakes his head and nips at my lower lip. "I want to *taste* you. Sixty-nine with me?"

For just a second, I pause. I wanted to give him all my attention and make him feel amazing. But at the same time, I also like the idea of us being equals and in this together. There is a power difference between us, after all. He's a rich, famous photographer and has the ability to make my career. But at this moment, I don't feel that. I just feel an insatiable yearning between two people who've been fighting an attraction for far too long.

"Sounds lush," I say with a grin. I'm eager to get him back in my mouth, but I can't deny that my cock strains even more at the idea of him finally touching me there. I shimmy out of the briefs, loving how eagerly he watches me.

"Come here," he murmurs, giving me a last kiss on the lips before encouraging me to turn around.

I fan out my robe so it's not in his face, then place my knees on either side of his head. I hiss as he glides his hand up and down my length before his lips wrap around the tip, sucking and licking it like a lollipop. His hot mouth feels so fucking good, and I give myself a second to just enjoy the sensation with my eyes closed.

But it's not long before I get the urge to swallow him again, so I wrap one hand around his base and take the rest of him as far down my throat as I can.

Our muffled moans are sinful, as are the slurping sounds filling the room. I shudder above him, doubting I'm going to be able to last long. But I feel like I've waited forever for this, even though it's only been a couple of weeks since we met. I've resisted this pull since I very first saw him.

I think it'll be okay if I give in quickly now. There will always be next time to take it slow.

Dear *lord*, let there be a next time.

After a few more minutes, I can't hold on any longer. Not when he's grunting and thrusting his cock down my throat, clearly loving every second like I am. I'm ready to swallow his load whenever he blows, but manners mean I have to release him for a moment and let him know.

"Oscar," I warn him as I gasp for air. "I'm getting close."

He also pulls his mouth off my cock but continues to stroke it vigorously. "Me too, baby. Do you want to come like this or facing each other?"

I would have been happy as we were, but all of a sudden, I know exactly what I want. I flick my robe and spin around, capturing his mouth with mine. His hand goes between us to encircle both our throbbing, slippery cocks, flying over them as we peak together.

"Oscar," I moan as my climax rushes over me. "Fuck, yes. *Oscar.*"

He throws his head back and cries out as he starts to come, his hand still frantically rubbing both of us. I look down, the sight of him creaming all over himself tipping me over the edge. I bury my face against his neck to muffle my scream as my cum mixes with his all over his hairy chest.

We're both trembling as we finally stop spurting.

I'm panting heavily and blinking my eyes back open as reality comes crashing down.

We really just did that. Is he going to be okay? Or is he going to run away again? I know I'm okay—I'm fucking fantastic. But it's hard to battle the anxiety that's creeping in when he ran away from our first real kiss barely half an hour ago.

Except before I can go off the rails, he slips his arms around my back and kisses the side of my neck sweetly. I don't care about the mess. I lower myself down onto his chest and allow myself to be cuddled fiercely.

"Baby," he murmurs, caressing the back of my neck.

I turn my head and kiss him gently. I've never been called 'baby' by a guy before. I always thought it seemed a bit cringe, but coming from Oscar in this moment, it's beautiful. I feel cherished by him.

He's definitely not running away.

"Are you okay?" I ask, looking into his hazel eyes.

"My back's fine," he assures me.

I roll my eyes and lightly smack his shoulder. "I mean *psychologically,* you numpty. Is that...are you feeling all right with what we just did?"

He sighs, and my guard goes up. But he shakes his head, and I needn't have worried.

"I'm not feeling all right. I'm feeling incredible. *You're* incredible."

I exhale and let out a little nervous laugh. "I thought you might have regrets."

He shakes his head again. "Definitely not. But I will if I don't clean myself up soon," he adds with a chuckle.

I look down and grin. "We did make quite a mess."

He strokes my hair fondly. "You're worth getting messy for. But I'd also like to look after you now and get us clean. Shower with me?"

I know I've got to stop comparing this wonderful man to my ex, but I was lucky if Chris even passed me a tissue after sex. Of course Oscar wants to take care of us properly. That's his style. And—oh my god—I was just lamenting back at his place that I'd never showered with another guy before. This is kind of amazing.

"I'd love to," I say seriously. But then I waggle my eyebrows. "And maybe we can go for round two whilst we're at it."

He barks out a laugh, then cups the side of my face fondly. "You whippersnapper. Maybe I'll make *you* come again, but this old man will need a little longer to recover."

I grin and kiss him sensually. "I'll wait all day for you to recover," I promise. "But I do want you again."

He swallows, something passing in his eyes that I can't quite decipher. But then it's gone, replaced by something warm and tender.

"You've got me," he says, repeating my words from earlier. And for now, at least, I believe him.

14

———

OSCAR

It's been a long time since I took a shower with someone else, but I don't think I've ever shared the experience with anyone quite as handsy as my Mr. Defries. He's like a slippery eel, his hands exploring every inch of my body under the pounding water as his mouth refuses to leave mine.

I manage to convince him to break away long enough to find my bottle of hair and body wash. I'm glad it's an all-in-one product, as getting him to concentrate is no easy task. Just as his lips don't want to be parted from mine, his hands are obsessed with fondling my cock and ass.

His youthful exuberance makes me laugh. I meant what I said about needing a bit of time to recuperate after that pretty spectacular orgasm. But that doesn't mean his touch is unwelcome. In fact, it's divine. He makes me feel as young and attractive as he is, which isn't bad for my ego at all.

But the truth is that I haven't got much to climax

with again just yet. *He* on the other hand, is raring to go. I pin him against the wall and jerk him off, kissing the shit out of him and making him yell my name as he blows all over me for a second time in under an hour.

A primal, savage part of me wishes that his ex could hear his unbridled pleasure. But fuck that guy. I don't really care what he thinks, only that Malyk is happy. And happy he seems, for real.

After his second orgasm, he's a lot more pliant, and allows me to wash us both properly. Then I get out and hand him a towel, but I get myself dried off a lot faster, so once I wrap it around my waist, I take his from him and help him finish the job.

"Thanks," he mumbles sleepily. I brush back one of his dark curls, and my heart aches. I've got a lot to think about, but in that moment, I just feel content down to my bones.

Back in our room, I find us both sweatpants to pull on then lay us back down on the bed. I'm glad we only made a mess of ourselves and not the sheets so we can easily be comfortable now without having to bother housekeeping.

He asked me if I was okay, and as he snuggles up against my chest, I have the urge to ask him the same thing. But he was very clear that this was what he wanted, so I don't labor the point.

I do feel a twinge of guilt, though. As we were getting changed, I *saw* that there was an impromptu catwalk going on by the pool. I'm pleased that Samson was down with them by Linny's side, so I know he's being looked after. Her people have obviously brought out some of the exclusive garments from next season's range, and the models looked to be having a whale of a time parading up and down to the music that's been turned up again.

Malyk should be networking. That's why he came all this way. But it turns out I'm a selfish old bastard and can't bear to part from him just yet. We still have the whole rest of the week for him to join in with the fun, and he already made such a good impression last night. I figure it's not so bad if I keep him to myself for a little longer.

But how much longer?

I chew on my lip as he dozes sweetly against my side. The retreat is for six more nights, but on the last day we'll travel back to my place. His flight to London is the day after that.

I resent that I can't simply live in the moment like he seems to and enjoy what's just happened. But part of why I keep so Zen these days is because I'm a planner. I know what my days, weeks, even the rest of my year is going to look like. I keep things simple. I haven't challenged myself for a long time.

Now Malyk has come into my life and uprooted everything like a hurricane.

I don't know what's going to happen when he has to go back home. How am I going to feel? I know I ran away from that kiss by the pool, so I don't have any right to feel as possessive as I do. I shouldn't really trust my judgment right now when I'm so all over the place. But I know why I ran. I was afraid I'd hurt him.

Now I'm so afraid to lose him I wrap my arms

around him just that little bit tighter and kiss the top of his head. *Fuck.* There are so many reasons that this won't work out—that it *shouldn't.* But my heart is thumping hard in my chest, and all I can think is that being with him just feels so right. He lights me up. He's daring and brilliant but also sweet and caring. And I'd be a liar if I didn't acknowledge that his beauty makes me want to only take photos of him for the rest of my career.

This must still be the orgasm pumping adrenaline through me or something. I'm delirious, thinking about forever like that. I don't know what's going to happen between us next week, let alone in years to come.

But it's as if this young man has bewitched me with a spell. Or more like I've been sleepwalking through life for the last several years, and he's come along and woken me up with a kiss like a prince in a fairy tale.

"Everything all right?" he asks, pulling me from my thoughts. I realize I'm still hugging him quite tightly and must have roused him from his nap. Not only have we just had sex, but we also had a late night drinking, and he's probably still jetlagged as he's not as used to flying around the world as I am. I release my grip and rub his arm.

"Sorry, baby," I say. I'm not sure how to explain my thoughts, though.

He hums. "Where did 'baby' come from?"

I raise my eyebrows, then look down at him. "Uh… I'm not sure. It just sort of happened. Do you mind?"

He grins shyly and wriggles against me. "I love it," he says softly. "No one's ever called me that before. It's sweet."

I relax and rest my cheek on the top of his head. I love him being my baby, but that seems too much to say out loud. Too fast. However, there *is* something different about being with someone so much younger. There's so much I want to do for him, to help him with and show him. But also…I love what he's doing to me in return. I feel like I've taken the world's best vitamins. Like I've been rejuvenated.

"Are you worrying about things?" he asks.

"What things?" I ask, hoping to gauge his mood before I try and sift through all my concerns. Because yeah, I am worrying a bit.

He shrugs and looks up at me fondly. "All the things that made you run off from the pool." His tone is warm and not accusatory, so I try not to feel bad. We are adults, after all. Talking our way through our feelings and problems is healthy.

"I am thinking," I admit. "About a lot of things. I keep coming back to the fact that if we both want to be together like this, it can't be wrong, right?"

"Right," he agrees firmly.

He moves so we're sitting side by side, but I still have my arm around his waist, and he's still snuggled up close, so I don't mind. In fact, if we're having a serious discussion, it's probably best that we can turn and look at each other more easily. Also, I'm not insensible to the fact that I'm the one with the money and connections. I don't want him feeling like he has to be submissive to me. I want us to be equals as much as we can.

"What we just shared was amazing, and I want more of it," he tells me boldly. There's a little brattishness in there as well that makes me smile. I like it when he gets bossy and demanding. "I know we started out pretending, but I don't see why we can't try being together for real when it feels this good."

I lick my lips and search his hazel eyes. "And at the end of the week?"

He shrugs and drops his eyes as he starts fiddling with the toggle on my sweatpants. "People have holiday romances, don't they? Maybe we just treat it like that. Something to enjoy in the here and now, and not worry about what happens afterward when we go back to real life."

It sounds so simple. So easy. But I don't do flings. I've only ever had long-term relationships. Perhaps this is another new thing he can share with me, that he can teach me. He's right. People have flings all the time. Who's to say there would even be a spark between us once we got back to real life? We both have unpredictable schedules, not to mention the whole living on different continents part. It might not work at all.

But this week could work. We're already sharing a room. It's a non-stop all-inclusive fabulous party with the added bonus that Malyk might even get an amazing career opportunity out of it. Our chemistry is obviously off the charts. Why not relax and just have some fun rather than trying to plan a whole relationship before it's even begun like I always seem to do? It's clearly not worked out in the past. Otherwise, I'd still be with Jerry or one of the other guys I dated in my twenties and thirties.

That makes me realize that I especially shouldn't

even think about tying Malyk down, as he's still in his early twenties with his whole life ahead of him. No. A fling sounds perfect. If I manage my expectations now, then we should be fine to part ways in a week's time. There's no sense worrying about what might be and ruining what little time we have together. I should jump in with both feet and enjoy every day as it comes.

"Malyk Defries," I say with a grin. "Will you be my fake boyfriend for real for the rest of the week and let me give you as many orgasms as possible in that time?"

He hums and places a finger on his chin, looking away like he's thinking about it.

I tickle his sides and make him shriek. In the kerfuffle, he ends up underneath me again, and the way he looks up at me is honestly breathtaking.

"I'd love that, Oscar," he says sincerely.

I capture his mouth for a searing kiss and grind my crotch against his through our sweatpants. I might be older than him, but I'm not *that* old. I start to swell, as does he.

Oh, yes. I think the next round of orgasms is in our immediate future.

Then maybe we might finally make it downstairs for breakfast.

Or maybe I'll see if it's possible to order room service.

15

MALYK

Well…that was a bit of a whirlwind.

In a good way. Don't get me wrong. But…wow.

Having not had sex since being with Chris, three orgasms in under two hours was earth-shatteringly good. I did completely fall asleep, though, after Oscar sucked me off and wanked all over me. This time he just wiped me down with a washcloth, but he still totally cleaned me up because he's a bloody gentleman.

I know there's a lot we're not saying. I know he's worrying enough for the both of us. But I'm trying my best to do what I said I would and live in the moment. This trip has only just begun, and it's already turning out to be the most incredible, unreal experience of my life. I feel like Alice falling into Wonderland.

So I've decided I can either question all the madness around me or pick up a croquet mallet and go join in with the tea party. We already have the flamingos, after all.

I'm grateful that Oscar wakes me in the early

evening. Jetlag and an orgasm overload are completely messing with my system, but we never ate all day, and I'm feeling a little queasy. I freshen up and pull on a pair of high-waisted, wide-leg olive-green trousers and a simple white singlet. I accessorize with small heeled brown boots, some gold jewelry, and just a little lip gloss. I don't need to make a grand entrance tonight, but I absolutely still want to look good.

But above all else, for the love of god, I need to eat.

Luckily, tonight is one of the buffets rather than a formal sit-down affair, so we don't have to wait around. The theme seems to be kind of Mediterranean and tapas, which is fine by me. I load up my plate on paella, spicy potatoes, chargrilled meats, and big fat olives. I make sure to get a full pint of water to start me off, but then the red wine is free flowing and gorgeous.

And all the while, Oscar is by my side, his hand, knee, or elbow touching me when at all possible. Just before we sat at our table in the dining hall, I spotted Chris and Frans across the room. Chris looked like he'd sucked on a slice of lemon right out of the sangria jug, but Frans gave me a sweet little wave, so I very obviously waved and blew him a kiss back. The sooner that boy ditches my scummy ex, the better.

But I can't worry about them. Not now. Not when Oscar keeps his hand on my knee all throughout our meal. Not when all sorts of people keep swinging by and making a point to talk to me. People who remember my name from yesterday, even when I don't really recall talking to them.

There's something electric in the air, I can tell.

Emmalina comes in just when I'm starting to feel human again and am slowing down to eat my food and sip my wine like a human being rather than a ravenous beast, so that's something I'm grateful for. I want to keep making a good impression in front of her. Speaking of ravenous beasts, I'm thrilled to see that Samson is still by her side, wagging his tail and looking like the star of the show. By the way people flock over to fuss him, he kind of is. I grin at Oscar and am glad to see that he's relieved.

"I saw her looking after him earlier, but I felt a bit bad," he says.

I shake my head. "Don't be," I insist. "He's having a blast, and we needed some alone time. We'll go give him extra attention when he and Emmalina are settled down. He's great. Don't worry. It's okay to look after yourself first and foremost sometimes."

He opens his mouth like he's going to protest. Then he sighs and cups his hand around my jaw. I love when he does that. "I was looking after *you*, so that I'll accept."

I frown at him, wanting to argue. He's actually allowed to take care of himself as well, as a matter of fact. But I'm interrupted by the guy who was dutifully toting around the contraption that shot out Emmalina's clay pigeons yesterday. He has a heavy-looking gift bag that he presents to Oscar. It's about the size of a piece of printer paper but a couple of inches deep, and I wonder what it could contain.

"Our host wanted you to have these," he says

somberly, even though the bag is pink and glittery with rainbow tissue paper poking out the top.

"Oh, um, thank you," Oscar says in confusion as he peeks inside the bag. Then his cheeks go bright red, and he sucks a breath in. Emmalina's guy is long gone, already winding through the tables back to her, but everyone else at our table has snapped their heads back toward Oscar.

"What is it?" I demand, trying to reach out and grab the goodie bag to see for myself. But he snatches it to his chest, then thinks better of his strategy and shoves it on the floor by his feet.

"Nothing," he says at a pitch just shy of a squeak. "I'll show you later."

I narrow my eyes at him but decide if it's got him this flustered, it has to be good, so I'll wait to look at it in private if that's what he wants. Still, he gives me absolutely no hints throughout the rest of dinner, and I'm burning with curiosity by the time people start drifting outside after dessert to watch the imminent fireworks display.

"Do you want to join them?" Oscar asks me, and for a second, I'm torn.

This is the whole reason I came here. To make an impression on Emmalina and her people. But—without wanting to sound conceited—I think she already knows who I am. I talked to plenty of people during dinner. Will it really matter if I'm not standing in the dark going ooh and ahh at the pretty lights?

Before I can answer, something nudges my thigh

and makes me jump. But then I realize it's Samson, and I laugh. "Hey, boy. What's up?"

He doesn't stick around, though. He just runs around and boops Oscar as well, his tail wagging, then runs off outside with a bark, presumably to find Emmalina.

It's probably crazy, but I can't help but feel he was trying to tell me something—or remind me of something. I only have a few days with Oscar. I don't want to waste them.

Besides, I want to know what's in that bloody bag.

"Let's go upstairs," I say meaningfully.

He nods and folds up the napkin from his lap neatly and places it on the table before reaching for Emmalina's present. I tingle with anticipation all the way up the stairs. I barely even register Chris walking by us at one point. My mind is consumed with thoughts of Oscar alone.

That is until we unlock the door to our room.

I almost crash into Oscar as he stops at the threshold. But then I see why and gasp as he begins laughing and shaking his head.

"I'm going to kill Linny," he says fondly.

I wasn't sure we even had cleaners in this place. I haven't seen them, but apparently, we do, because the bed's been made all nicely. That's not what startled us, though.

The duvet, carpet, and furniture tops have all been covered with pink, white, and red rose petals. The same style hurricane jars and pillar candles that were burning outside yesterday evening have been placed around the room. There's a sweet smell in the air and gentle instrumental music playing from a Bluetooth speaker on the dresser.

"Are we in the right room?" I ask slightly nervously.

"Ohh yes," Oscar confirms. He closes the door behind us and hands over the mysterious bag.

I eagerly rush to the bed and sit down in a flurry of petals, pulling off the rainbow tissue paper. My mouth drops open, and for a second I just stare at what's inside. Then I begin laughing.

A three-pack of different flavored lubes. A pretty big box of condoms. A brand-new vibrating dildo still in its box—purple and sparkly. Some kind of double Fleshlight that would enable two people with dicks to fuck face-to-face. Fluffy handcuffs and a blindfold. Chocolate body paint complete with a fancy brush.

"Oh my fucking god," I cackle as Oscar sits beside me, also grinning. "I get why you didn't want to share this at the dinner table. This is hilarious!"

He slips his hand over my thigh, and suddenly it becomes a lot less funny and about a thousand percent sexier.

"Do you want to use any of it?" he murmurs.

"Now?" I ask, licking my lips.

He nods. "If that's what you want."

My heart is beating really fast. We literally spent all morning making love, and I slept all afternoon in his arms in this very bed. But this is something different. A step up. Do I want to allow myself to be that vulnerable with him?

Yes. I think I do.

"Can we keep it simple?" I ask, selecting the lube and condoms. "Oh, um, but also maybe this," I add shyly, picking up the pot of chocolate paint.

He grins as he leans in and captures my mouth in a filthy kiss. "Do you want to be the painter or the canvas?"

I gulp. I don't know why I'm so nervous. I think it's because I want this so badly. If we're only going to have a few days and nights together, I want every time we fuck to be amazing.

But this will be the first time he's going to be inside me.

We talked earlier and already established that we're both versatile when it comes to topping and bottoming. But in this moment, I really want him to take care of me like he promised. He's been so very good at it so far, after all.

Toward the end of our relationship, Chris made me feel selfish when I asked for what I wanted in the bedroom, so it's difficult for me to look Oscar in the eye. But as soon as I do, I see so much affection and tenderness there it gives me confidence. He just *asked* me what I want. It's okay to respond honestly.

I look down at the chocolate and fiddle with the lid. "Maybe you could stretch me. Eat me out with this, then fuck me."

He groans and kisses my neck, making me shudder and gasp. "We did skip dessert," he says playfully against my skin. "I like this plan."

I place my hands on his chest and rub them against

his pecs, shoulders, and biceps. I'm still a little uncertain. "Yeah?"

"Yeah," he replies. "You just lie back and think of England, okay? Or Wales," he adds with a chuckle. "Let me take care of you."

I bite my lip. I don't want to be a pillow princess—it's not really my style. In fact, usually, I'm pretty wild in the sack. But right now, the idea of letting Oscar take charge seems lovely.

"Okay," I say with an impish air as I paw at his shirt buttons. "But at least let me help you out of all these unnecessary clothes."

"Deal," he says.

Rose petals swirl everywhere as we stumble around, helping each other get undressed. Some stick to our dampening skin, making me giggle. It's funny but also pretty sexy.

Soon enough, we're naked again, but there's something different in the air compared to this morning. It's more charged somehow. More urgent. Oscar kisses me as we both stand at the foot of the bed. Then he rubs up and down my arms, nuzzling our noses together.

"Lie down for me, beautiful," he murmurs. "On your front. Show me that gorgeous ass."

I bite my lip, but it doesn't contain my grin. I give him a quick peck on the lips before crawling over the bed, looking over my shoulder at him so I can watch him watching my bum. My cock swings between my legs, throbbing in anticipation.

His hands are by his sides, giving him a cool, casual

air as usual. But the way his dick is already beading precum suggests he's anything but chill.

I lie down and bring one of my knees up higher toward my hip, so it pulls my cheeks apart a little, inviting him in. I rest my chin on my shoulder and bat my eyelashes at him, hoping I'm doing a good job of seducing him. He's a pretty sure thing at this stage, but I want him to feel as desired as he's making me feel.

He wets his lips, studying my body and making me shiver. He then tilts his head and finally lifts his gaze to meet mine.

"Can I photograph you?"

My breath hitches. Like this? I've been super careful to never send a nude or a dick pic in my life, even when I was a desperate, horny teenager. I'd hate for one reckless decision to jeopardize my career in modeling.

But I think about where I am. On a bed covered in rose petals. My most intimate parts are hidden. It's just my arse on display. And this is one of the greatest photographers in the business.

If he wants to capture this moment between us, I bet it will be sensational.

I nod shyly, then watch as he retrieves his camera. This is the first time he's gotten it out the whole trip. He takes his time to fiddle with the lens and play around with the candles, then gets out a small ring light to attach to his equipment. We've both lost our erections somewhat, but that's okay. A serene kind of calm has befallen the room.

He starts clicking away, shifting his body this way and that, his entire focus on me. For a while, I get to marvel at his naked form, but then he starts giving me instructions to look in various directions, and I fall into a kind of trance, somewhere in between my usual modeling state of concentration and a blissed-out meditation. After a while, my eyes drift closed, finding the noise of the shutter over the ambient music oddly soothing.

When the clicking stops and I hear him place his camera down on the dresser, I'm almost dozing. But when he runs his hand up the back of my thigh and over the swell of my arse, I take in a deep, slow breath and open my eyes.

"Hey," I murmur sleepily.

"Hey," he rasps back.

"Did you get any good ones?"

He smiles and shakes his head like I'm incorrigible. "Far too many to choose from, I'm sure. You take my breath away."

I have to look away as I swallow the lump that threatens to rise in my throat. I've wanted to model since I was a teenager. I thought getting signed and doing my first shoot would be the biggest validating moments for me. But it turns out it's in this room, with no audience and photos no one else will probably ever see, that I feel the most authentic. Like I've really arrived.

I reach out and interlace our fingers, kissing his knuckles. "So do you," I assure him. Just the sight of him makes me dizzy. We might not have known each other long, but in that time, we've been through so much and learned a lot about each other.

He's becoming very important to me. And the thought of losing him so fast isn't something I want to dwell on.

So I don't. I push myself up slowly with my free hand, keeping my eyes locked on his as I lean in and capture his mouth, dragging the lower lip through my teeth. "Do you still want dessert?" I practically purr.

"Fuck, yes," he growls before kissing me hard and wrapping his hand around my cock. It's already coming back to life as I've woken up, but it springs in his grasp, eager and willing. "Lie down, beautiful. Pull your knees apart. Relax."

I'm not sure I'm going to be able to really relax with how excited I am, but I do as he asks, giving him easy access to my hole. I have a pillow under my head, and I close my eyes, wanting to focus purely on the feeling of what's to come. As if reading my mind, he slips a silky fabric over my forehead.

"Is this okay?" Oscar asks as he settles the blindfold from the goodie bag over my eyes.

I exhale and nod. "Amazing." I don't want to wear it when we fuck, but for now, it's perfect.

I'm anticipating the intimate touch, but I still jump a little when the wet brush strokes over my entrance, sticky with the chocolate. I moan and try not to wriggle as Oscar caresses my bum cheek with one hand and paints me thoroughly with the other.

There's a little pause, and then his tongue takes one long swipe up my crack.

"Fucking fuck," I grunt, and grind my hardening cock against the bedding. Oscar hums, clearly amused, but then he's got two hands gripping my arse as he starts to lick and kiss my hole, his tongue probing against the tight ring of muscle.

I pant and undulate against the bed, my cock desperate for friction as he takes his time lapping every morsel of sweetness up. His tongue breaches me over and over, gradually loosening me up. Once I'm completely clean, he switches to the strawberry-flavored lubricant (or so I assume from the new scent that fills the room), then he pushes two of his fingers inside me.

I cry out at the initial burn, but it quickly fades. "Do you like that?" he asks, kissing my arse cheek.

I nod frantically, my skin damp with perspiration and my cock leaking between me and the duvet. "So good, Oscar. God, I want you to fuck me so badly."

He chuckles. "Patience, little brat," he says in a teasing voice. "Such a diva."

"I *am* the star of the show, you know," I announce. But then he retaliates by crooking his fingers and finding my prostate, stroking that hypersensitive nub, and making me jerk and moan in pleasure. "Fuck, *yes*. Like that," I tell him.

"I think I can do better than that," he says, and the next thing I know, his fingers withdraw, and my hole is left fluttering and desperate. I tear off the blindfold with a gasp, needing to see what's happening.

He's rolling a condom down his length, then grins at me as he rubs extra lube over it before fondling my crack to make it extra slippery. "Are you ready, beautiful?"

I push up onto my hands and knees, practically

shoving my arse back into him. "I'm so fucking ready," I say, making him laugh.

But then he's angling the tip so it's pushing through my hole, and I cry out in pleasure. It might be a bit of a stretch, but I want him so badly. I love being on all fours for him, taking him as far as he can go. Before long, he's bottomed out, and he bends down and wraps himself around me, kissing my neck and cheek until I turn my head enough for our mouths to meet.

"You feel fucking amazing," he tells me reverently.

"So do you," I agree wholeheartedly. "Fuck me hard. Make me come."

He kisses me brutally again, then kneels up and grabs hold of my hips. "Fuck, Malyk," he grunts as he starts to piston in and out of me. "You're so beautiful."

The way he says it makes me feel powerful. He called me a goddess yesterday. And here he is, worshipping me in the most intimate way possible.

I throw my head back and let out a long guttural sound. Every time his cock slams against my prostate I see fireworks I'm sure are way better than the ones now exploding outside. But I can't deny that the crackles and booms coming through the glass don't add to the ceremonial experience. This is my very own coronation.

"Oscar, fuck!" I cry out. "Touch me. Make me come."

I could stroke myself off, but where's the fun in that? Especially when he growls, "Yes, baby, *yes*," and grabs a firm hold of my cock, jerking frantically, matching the rhythm of our hips.

I dig my fingers into the bed, getting fistfuls of the

duvet as I rock back and forth, impaling myself on him again and again. His hand flies over my cock, the slippery sound of it mingling with the slapping of our skin and animalistic grunts. I can taste the sweet strawberry and chocolate scents in the air as well as the distinct masculine musk coming from our pounding bodies. It's primal but beautiful, and as much as I want it to last, I can feel myself rushing over the precipice to greet my climax.

"Oscar!" I yell as I start to blow my load, struggling for breath as my vision blacks out. The orgasm almost stops my heart as it slams into me. He wrings every last drop from me, milking my cock and pummeling my arse until he goes rigid. I feel him throbbing inside me, his load spilling inside the condom.

He gradually slows, thrusting into me with a tenderness as we both ride out our high. Then he drops down and hugs me, pulling us against the mattress as he spoons me from behind, his cock softening inside me.

"Fuck," I rasp, blinking, even though the candlelight isn't any brighter than it was a moment ago. My heart is also racing, and I'm panting like I've just run a hundred-meter sprint. I find his hand and cradle it against my chest. "Not bad for an old man."

There's a beat where I'm not sure he heard me right. Then he roars with laughter and buries his face against my neck. I grin, feeling pretty pleased with myself. I love a good hard fuck, but it's even better when it's not too serious. That was some of the best fun I've ever had with a man.

Plus, the way he's hugging me now and kissing my

neck still makes me feel beautiful and cherished. He's the best of all worlds.

I don't know how I'm supposed to get any work done this week. Because as far as I'm concerned, there's nothing that could drag me away from this bed now.

16

OSCAR

"Come on, it'll do you good," I urge Malyk.

He's pouting at me and very naked on the bed the next morning, but I'm throwing my older and wiser card down onto the table.

We have to leave this room and take a break from the orgasms. We need some fresh air and food. The maid *definitely* needs to help us out. And I've abandoned my dog to my friend for twenty-four hours now. A walk is what we all need.

Even if the temptation to sink back into that bed and allow Malyk to suck my cock like he so desperately wants to is *strong*.

But I hold on to my resolve. Malyk came here to network, and as confident as I am that he's already made a good impression on Emmalina, I'm not going to hide him away in this room for the rest of the week.

He flops and huffs dramatically. *"Fine,"* he concedes. "I'll shower. But only if you join me."

I laugh as he waggles his eyebrows. Now that, I can't

resist, especially if it'll ultimately get him to do what I want.

A lot of suds and two orgasms later, we're dressed and rejuvenated, heading down for breakfast. This time we don't get interrupted and are able to actually enjoy our food. We both stick to juice to drink, however. After two pretty eventful days, I think we can probably wait for another buzz until tonight or even tomorrow.

Samson comes bounding over to us with Linny in tow. The smug look on her face confirms to me that she knew all about the gift bag and our room's sexy makeover. "Good morning, boys," she drawls as she places a hand on the back of my chair and leans over us. "I take it you had a good day yesterday. Day *and* night," she adds with a smirk.

"Delightful," says Malyk with a Cheshire cat grin, not embarrassed at all. "Thank you for the pressies."

She winks and sips from her Champagne saucer. "Did you use everything?" she asks innocently.

Malyk scoffs as I feel my cheeks heat up. We're not *that* good of friends. She doesn't need any details. But he's got an equally innocent look on his face as he volleys a reply. "Not yet," he says, sounding vaguely scandalized. "We've got to leave something spicy for the other nights."

I groan and cover my face, but he squeezes my knees sweetly.

"Oh, poor Oscar," Linny cries and rubs my shoulder, but her chuckle is all devilment. "He's out of practice. You'll have to help him get fit again," she tells Malyk, who looks positively gleeful at the suggestion.

"Oh, I've got many ideas," he says, dragging a finger along my thigh.

"Samson," I say loudly to my dog, who immediately barks and wags his tail. "Would you like to go for a walk?"

"Fine, I can take a hint," Emmalina says with a wave of her hand. "You kids have fun. Don't get so distracted that you're eaten by bears."

Malyk's face drops as she walks away, and he snaps his head toward me. "There aren't really bears around here, are there?"

I stand and try not to smile or laugh. "You'll just have to behave so you don't find out, won't you?"

"That's no fun," he grumbles as he also gets to his feet.

Everything about this young man is fun, though. Even a walk through the grounds has me beaming so much my face aches. He's such lively company, always full of stories or ready to play fetch with my dog with some old stick he's picked up off the ground.

"So what's on the itinerary for the rest of the week?" he asks.

He's been quite preoccupied with the schedule. It doesn't usually bother me because I just wear the same clothes to everything and roll with whatever activity or event is taking place. But it's different for him, I do understand. He has to organize outfits and make sure he's getting noticed by the right kinds of people.

So I decide now's the time to stop being vague about it and finally find that PDF with all the details on it that got sent out weeks ago. It takes me a while, as

Linny's wi-fi doesn't reach out this far, but eventually, I'm able to download the thing onto my phone.

"Okay, tonight is the big games evening. We'll be put into teams and challenged with completing the most ridiculous tasks."

"Like what?" he asks.

I shrug. "Dirty charades. Pin the dong on the model. Things involving balloons and whipped cream. Beer pong—but with Champagne, of course. Twister. Then everything usually devolves into karaoke." I wink at him. "The point of tonight is to see who's good at letting loose and isn't so worried about looking perfect."

He visibly relaxes. "Oh, good. Because I'm *very* competitive."

I grin, my heart swelling. Of course he is. I was worried he'd be one of the prissy guests, as there are always a few. They just want to sit back and be stunning, too afraid to get messy or silly.

I can already see that Malyk has gold medals in his eyes, and I kind of love him for it.

I mean…I love that about him. I mean…

I clear my throat and stop trying to work out what exactly it is I love in this moment.

"Tomorrow is the nighttime pool party where Emmalina likes to show off beachwear that won't even see the runway until at least next spring. You'll really want to get in on that action if you can. I'll also be photographing that one along with a couple of the other guys. Sometimes the pictures are so good they make it into catalogs or campaigns."

His eyes are going as big as saucers as he takes in

everything I'm saying. He's rightly worked out that this is one of the events to pay attention to.

"I'll make sure to speak to Linny and get you in something she loves," I tell him, bumping shoulders as we carry on walking through the forest, Samson bounding around our legs.

Malyk nudges me back with a shy smile. "Thanks," he says.

I glance over the next couple of days. "Things calm down a bit, then. There's a hike, a barbecue, things like quizzes and a relaxed art class with live models, of course. Then the final night is the big masquerade ball," I say, closing the app on my phone and putting it back in my pocket. "That one's quite a big deal." In previous years, I've left before all the pomp and ceremony that usually entails, but this year I have a feeling I'll be sticking around.

However, I realize that Malyk has stopped walking, and I turn and look at him in confusion. His face is horrified when I'd be sure he'd be excited.

"A ball?" he repeats.

"Yeah," I say with enthusiasm, as if that might encourage him. "Like the kind you see on TV on those British period dramas." I do my best at a bow and extend my hand to him. "May I have this dance, good sir?" I ask in a very poor attempt at a posh English accent.

But when he continues to look shocked—in fact, now he's practically looking *upset*—I stand up and realize I've definitely missed something here.

"Malyk, what's wrong?" I ask with genuine concern.

I step closer to him, then it's my turn to be horrified as a tear rolls down his cheek. "Fuck!" I cry and rush to grab either side of his shoulders. Samson rubs his head against his leg with a whimper, then sits at his feet. "Have I said something? Malyk, talk to me."

"A ball?" he croaks out as more tears fall. "Like a proper one with fancy suits and dresses and masks?" I nod, still baffled. I honestly thought this would be the sort of thing he'd love.

Then I finally understand, and I could kick myself. Hard.

"I don't have anything to wear to something like that!" he says, sounding genuinely panicked. "I don't have fancy couture. I don't have a ballgown hidden somewhere in my luggage. Oh, god. I'm going to look like a joke. Everyone will know I don't belong. That I could never fit in with people who have actual money. I'm going to humiliate myself!"

"Malyk, baby, shh shh shh!" I plead as I pull him into a fierce hug. "What are you talking about? You belong here more than half the other people who have been coming to Honeyrock for years! You can't *buy* talent and beauty like you have. But you know what you can buy?" I lean back to look at him and pause to brush the tears from his face that I hate with a passion, even though he still looks gorgeous as he cries. "Clothes," I tell him when he doesn't answer my question. "We can take a car and go back to the city and get you whatever outfit you desire."

His face threatens to crumple again as his lips tremble. "I can't *afford* that," he whispers. "I can't fool people like this. They know what's designer and what's been cobbled together from the high street."

My heart breaks, and I'm already shaking my head before he's even finished talking. "Baby," I say kindly. "I told you. *I'm* looking after you for this whole trip. If you need couture, I'm buying you couture." He opens his mouth to protest, but I gently cup the side of his face to encourage him to stop. "No, this is my fault. I didn't warn you that you'd basically need a Bridgerton ensemble. It didn't occur to me because I'm a simple old man who lives in his jeans."

Like I'd hoped, that gets a small, wet laugh from him. "You're not old," he mumbles, but there's still a hint of that brattiness that I'm already so fond of.

"And you're not defined by what's in your bank account," I say firmly. "Not to me." I jerk my thumb back toward the house. "Yeah, some people there might be dicks about it, but we don't care about them. Some people could drop thousands of dollars on an outfit and still look painfully boring. You could wear the shit out of a brown paper bag, because you have *style*. But why not also help that with some nice clothes? You turned the most heads on the first night, so you're damned well going to do the same on the last night, too."

I hadn't meant to give quite such an impassioned speech, but I don't regret it. Not when he bites his lip and his wet eyes light up with the tiniest glimmer of hope. "I don't want to take advantage of you," he says quietly.

I scoff. "You could *never,*" I insist. "This is my gift.

Can't fake boyfriends buy their fake boyfriends gifts out of the blue?"

That gets another little laugh out of him, and he wipes his eyes and takes a shuddery breath. "Maybe one day I'll pay you back," he suggests.

I frown and rub his arms. "You'll do no such thing. I don't give gifts to expect anything in return. It would be my pleasure to give this to you and see you shine. You deserve it."

He hesitates for a few moments longer, but then he nods and leans back into me for another hug, which I'm more than happy to provide.

"I'm sorry I let you down, but I'm going to make it right," I promise.

"Thank you," he says with a sigh.

I stroke his back and realize I'm not being entirely selfless.

If I buy him something beautiful, he can take it home to London with him. That way, he'll still have a piece of me with him, even if we're an ocean apart.

17

MALYK

As the skyscrapers of New York City begin to grow around us, I wonder yet again what the hell I'm doing. Who am I? What has my life become?

Although the more of the complimentary Champagne I drink in the back of this limo Emmalina organized for us, the easier it is to accept Oscar's very generous offer. Strange, I know. But I figure I can fight him and feel guilty, or roll with it. We only have a couple more days together, and I want to make the most of them. The bubbly's helping to remind me of that.

It's funny that I'm actually not at all mad at him. I could easily be. He neglected to tell me an enormous detail that really could have fucked me over. But I understand how it wouldn't have even been on his radar. He doesn't see parties the same way I do in the slightest. For him, they're something to endure. For me, they're an important part of my work.

No. I'm mad at myself. If I wasn't in all this terrible debt, I could be investing in the future of my career. I wouldn't feel so ashamed in front of these people who are already on the inside and have such power over me.

But ultimately, I've decided I can spiral and feel awful about it or accept Oscar's offer to take care of me.

I'm not a greedy person. However, I can't deny that I'm slightly dying inside from euphoria at the idea of an all-expenses paid shopping spree in New York. I feel like I've accidentally stepped into a Sex and the City episode, and I don't want to leave.

I expect to go to one of the big department stores, but instead the limo pulls up in front of a small boutique. The name *'L'homme'* is painted in gold on the window, and even from the car, I can already see so many fine fabrics.

The fact that Oscar knows I would never want to wear a regular black suit makes me feel all tingly inside. He even asked if I wanted to wear a dress or some other option, but I feel a suit is the right call for this particular event. I love that thinking outside the box came so naturally to him, though.

"Wow," I whisper as the driver kills the engine.

"I might not have an adventurous fashion sense myself," Oscar says, sounding proud, "but I do know a thing or two about shopping in this town."

I bite my lip and turn to him in excitement. "This is like a dream," I say.

He winks. "We're just getting started, baby."

He's not kidding.

When we step inside the store, it's oddly quiet and still until a beautiful Black man with dreads down to his waist appears with a clap of his hands. "Mr. Defries," he says, his American accent smooth like butter. "We've been expecting you. Welcome."

What? I blink and turn to Oscar for an explanation. He grins. "Emmalina pulled in a favor," he says, like it's no big deal.

"Have we got the place to ourselves?" I ask in disbelief, looking between him and our host.

"Of course, darling," he says with a wave of his fingers like he's a fairy sprinkling magic dust. "My name is Briceson, and I'll be taking care of you today with my team. Can I offer you some refreshments? Champagne, perhaps?"

I'm going to have to detox for a month when I get home. I've barely recovered from the games evening last night (which my and Oscar's team naturally won). But how can I say no? As they say—when in Rome—or downtown Manhattan, in this case.

"Thank you," I say genuinely. I don't feel the need to perform in here like I have been at all the parties. I don't need to be sassy or flirty. I just want to be humble and grateful, absorbing it all in because I'm damned sure I'm never going to experience anything like this again anytime soon.

The walls are exposed brick, and the floor is polished wood. The lighting is like something out of a theater rather than a shop, and above our heads hangs an artistic flurry of autumn leaves. Then there are the clothes themselves. The displays are minimal and only show one of each design, so I have a feeling there's a lot more out the back than anyone ever sees. But the patterns are exquisite in all colors of the rainbow. The cuts and styles are so unusual. I just want to try everything on all at once.

Oscar explained that the ball isn't actually some Bridgerton cosplay or anything. People take inspiration from historical pieces, but the intention is more to look fabulous than period accurate. Which is good because I know eff all about history.

I know about clothes, though.

Briceson obviously agrees, which makes me feel amazing. "You have a good eye," he comments as he comes back. He's got a bottle of Champagne in an ornate silver bucket in one hand and two tall glasses dangling from the other. He juts his chin at the teal blazer with a subtle tropical bird print that I'm currently examining.

I shake my head and step away, looking around the store again. "Everything's so lush," I say in awe. "I don't know where to begin."

"Take as long as you like," Oscar encourages me. He's sat himself down in a purple velvet armchair, and it seems like he's settled in for the afternoon. "And no looking at price tags," he threatens me, but there's such affection to his tone it warms my heart even as I blush. I'm still not used to being spoiled, but if it's coming from Oscar, I'm learning to accept it.

"Why don't we get started with this one?" Briceson suggests, handing me a glass of bubbly and nodding toward the teal. "Then see where that takes us."

"Sounds like a plan," I concur.

We pair that jacket with a black pair of trousers and a white shirt, but sadly the fit doesn't quite work with my long body. Briceson offers to tailor it, but it would take so much work it wouldn't be done in time for the ball on Friday, so with a heavy heart, I have to walk away from it.

We try several more designs, including a crazy powder-blue crop top blazer that I wear by itself and matching wide, flowing pants and a sparkly white belt. We all agree that it's not right for the ball, but Oscar insists that I put it aside anyway to take home as a bonus extra. I feel guilty—I agreed to just *one* outfit. But Briceson helps him gang up on me, so I reluctantly accept the gift with a secret happiness glowing inside me.

It's not about the money (because I'm being good and not looking at a single price tag). It's about the fact that someone other than my mother actually gives a damn about me and wants me to have nice things. To feel special and treasured.

I never want this feeling to end, even though it must in a few days. So I do accept the powder-blue ensemble, knowing that every time I wear it back in London, I'll have a little bit of Oscar close to my heart.

After an hour or so, we take a break. Briceson's people appear like helpful mice in a Disney movie, tidying up the clothes that we've discarded and bringing us plates of fancy, delicious sandwiches and other finger food, as well as more Champagne, of course. I sigh happily. It doesn't matter that we haven't found the right look yet. I'm having so much fun.

And I'm having it with Oscar.

As Briceson speaks with one of his guys, I take a

moment to reach over and squeeze Oscar's hand. "Thank you," I murmur sincerely. "This is incredible, honestly. I'll never forget it."

He lifts my hand and gently kisses the backs of my fingers. "You're welcome. But it's Emmalina you really should be thanking. She pulled all the strings."

I give him a one-armed shrug. "And I will, absolutely. But you're the one who made it happen. You're the one who's here with me."

He leans in and gives my cheek a chaste kiss, but it's so romantic my heart still melts. I hear a dramatic yet wistful sigh, and we break apart. Briceson is watching us like we're a Hallmark movie, and he's got love hearts in his eyes.

"Completely adorable," he says, shaking his head, then sipping from his own fresh Champagne flute. "Where do I get a man to look at me like that? Just… picture perfect."

I smile shyly and glance back at Oscar, who caresses the side of my face.

"Malyk does take one hell of a photo," he confirms.

"He certainly will once we nail this ensemble, sugar. I've still got plenty of ideas. Don't you worry. In fact…"

He rises from the chaise lounge where he's been perched with a frown on his face. He places his glass down on a display covered in mannequin hands holding beaded bracelets and necklaces, before venturing to the back of one of the displays. He pulls out an iridescent purple jacket and matching skinny trousers. Just by looking at them, my heart leaps with hope. We've had to eliminate several gorgeous options because they—like the teal—would take too long to alter to fit my body. Some of them just wouldn't work even with all the altering in the world, as it would turn them into completely different garments. But this?

This has promise.

"No shirt," Briceson declares, twirling around the store and plucking a slim, shimmering black scarf from a display that looks like tree branches. Then he spins again, eyeing up the shoe rack. "Or socks. Try these."

He selects a shiny black pair with delicate embroidery a bit like Paisley on the toe. It's also got a decent heel, which gives me a thrill. After getting Oscar's enthusiastic approval for being however tall I damn well want to be, I've been wanting to explore other shoe options more.

The dressing room doesn't have a mirror. I've been witnessing Oscar's and Briceson's reactions when I pull back the curtain before I see the outfit myself. So I'm nervous as I get changed into this new combination. It certainly feels good. The fit is almost perfect, and the material has a dozen different colors running through it over the purple. It's cool and soft to the touch, like marble.

I feel like a work of art.

I take a breath, bracing myself before the big reveal, watching both their faces for their reactions, but mostly Oscar's. It's him I want to impress the most. I want him to be so proud of the date on his arm. He's the one who's got me this far, and I want to shine like a diamond to prove he didn't bet on the wrong horse.

But for a second, neither of them moves a muscle,

and my stomach drops. I was so sure this would be the one, but maybe I was wrong. However, then Briceson whistles and shakes his head, holding up his hands.

"Girl, I am *done.* That's it. Close up shop. We finished for the day."

"Malyk," Oscar utters, and to my surprise and mild horror, his voice cracks with emotion. I stay still and watch him as he rises to his feet and carefully walks over to me, like I'm extremely fragile and expensive. He touches my shoulders lightly, then cups my face. "You're going to blow them all away."

He encourages me to turn and look at my reflection, and I can't help but gasp.

It's everything I dreamed it would be and more.

This person belongs at that fancy house with all those important people. This person matters.

"Oh my god," I rasp, embarrassed that my eyes are wet, but there's not much I can do about it. "Briceson, it's incredible."

"Sweetie, I know," he says in a blasé manner, coming over to fuss with my cuffs. "Yes, okay. We can take this in a fraction here, and then…"

He snaps his fingers, and one of his people appears from nowhere with a pin cushion. He starts fitting me for slight alterations, but unlike all the others, these are so minor they can be done over the next couple of days. They also won't change the overall shape of the suit too much. But they just give it that little something extra to make it absolutely perfect. The devil's in the details, and having come this far, I'm all for getting the final look exactly right.

I look at Briceson working for a while, but then my gaze is drawn to Oscar. He's watching me with such pride and warmth that it kind of takes my breath away. Our eyes stay locked, but it doesn't get uncomfortable. It's like I'm staring into his soul, and he's staring into mine. My heart wants to burst it's so full. I've never felt this amazing with another man, ever. Not even close. It's like when we're together, I'm complete. Whole. Full.

Is this what love feels like?

18

OSCAR

Malyk is quiet on the drive home. He doesn't seem upset, just thoughtful, so I don't push him to talk. Besides, he keeps his hand in mine for the entire journey, his thumb rubbing calming little circles against my skin, so whatever's on his mind I hope it's not too serious.

I'm pleased he didn't fight me on getting him his clothes in the end. I thought for sure he'd kick up a fuss about the extra blue one, but it was so fun I couldn't let him leave it, and I was thrilled that he accepted it with grace.

He deserves nice things in life. It's my honor to be able to give him some.

We left both the suits with Briceson to make minor adjustments. They should be ready to collect on Friday in time for the ball and then to take home with us on Saturday.

But then Sunday, Malyk will *actually* be flying home and...

And I don't know if I'll ever see him again.

I'm grateful for the quietness as I sift through my own thoughts. I wish that he lived here. Then we could date and see where this thing between us goes. There's not much chance for growth when there's going to be an ocean between us. I guess we can stay in touch long distance, of course. But will that be enough?

I'm starting to think it won't be. That this isn't just a flash in the pan or a vacation fling. I knew it wouldn't be. That's not how I operate. It's simply not in my nature.

When I fall, I fall hard and fast and with my whole damned heart.

But even thinking back on my past relationships, this is different still. More, somehow. I've never met anyone like Malyk Defries, and I can't imagine not having him in my life.

What does that mean? Would I move to London? It's an amazing city, but it's not home. New York is. And could I really expect Malyk to give up *his* home when I don't want to? Especially for a relationship that's as new and fragile as a baby deer wobbling on its skinny legs. Not that he could even afford to.

Well, that part's moot. I'd pay for his flight and invite him to move in with me. But that's so fast we'd both get whiplash. I'd be insane to even consider it.

Still, when we arrive back at Honeyrock and have to get out of the limousine, it hurts me to let go of his hand. Like even just that amount of distance is too painful.

Fuck. This is a mess.

Emmalina has Samson until the evening. I'd planned on picking him up again right away, but instead, I lead Malyk back up to our room, close the door, and sit next to him on the edge of the bed. We stay still for a few moments with his hand cradled in mine.

"Talk to me," I say eventually.

"I don't want to leave you," he whispers immediately.

His eyes are fixed on a point somewhere around his knees, but I can see they're glassy with tears, and I hate that. This was supposed to be a fun day. But I can't say I blame him. A lump is already rising in my throat as I think of how to reply.

"Neither do I," I say. "You're amazing."

"So are you," he says, turning to look me in the face. "I've never felt like this about anyone."

"Nor have I. And that means twice as much because I'm twice as old as you." It's supposed to be a joke, but he doesn't even crack a smile, and my own laugh is rueful.

The years between us really don't matter. The miles will, though.

"Hey, come on," I urge him, trying to take charge and change the mood. "We said that would be okay. That we'd just enjoy the time we *do* have together."

He shrugs and looks away again. "I'm just sad," he says. "But…maybe you could come visit sometime?" He blinks, hope in his eyes once more, and I hug him to my side.

"I'd love that," I tell him honestly.

It's a Band-Aid and we both know it, but it's enough to fool ourselves for a little while.

"Come here," I murmur as I kick my shoes off. He does the same and lets me guide him up the bed to lie down in my arms. He clings to me, and our limbs tangle around each other. I kiss his curly hair, then rest my cheek on his forehead. "Maybe you'll come out here for work," I also suggest. "We know Emmalina likes you."

"She has an office in London, though," he says heavily. Then he takes in a deep breath and shakes himself. "But yeah, you're right. It's not like we're going to vanish from each other's lives. And this week will always be special no matter what."

"Absolutely," I agree.

We hold each other's gazes for a few moments before our mouths naturally drift together. The kiss is full of yearning, strong and sensual. Despite the dozens of kisses we've shared over the past few days, somehow this one is different again. More meaningful.

I hate that we've still got a few days to go before we have to part ways and melancholy has already descended upon us, but I think that just proves the intensity of our feelings. He's a remarkable young man, and it's hard for me not to imagine a way that we could be together.

Instead, I lose myself in the here and now and in him. My hands find their way under his shirt and skim over his beautifully smooth skin. I feel his heart beating and the breath as it fills his lungs. He's so alive and full of energy. There's a bright spark that even our sadness can't extinguish for long.

He caresses the side of my face and nips at my lower lip. "Make love to me, Oscar," he whispers.

"Of course, baby," I tell him back. There's nothing I want more in that moment than to show him the depth of my feelings.

Because I'm pretty sure it's love.

We snuggle down on the bed, lying facing each other just kissing for a while. My hand is still under his shirt, stroking his back, but there's no great urgency to it. I want us to take our time, to stretch out this moment together.

He squeezes my hip and then reaches around to grope my ass. I smile against his mouth. "Do you want something, sweetheart?"

"You."

I nuzzle our noses together. "You've got me."

But he shakes his head. "I want to top you," he explains. "I mean, I want to be inside you. I thought you could maybe ride me."

I shiver and groan, kissing him slowly. "That sounds wonderful," I say sincerely.

Honestly, we've had good fun with all of Linny's gifts, but right now, I just want to keep things simple. So far, I've topped him each time, but I love the idea of him inside me.

And yeah, riding him sounds perfect. I want to protect him and cradle him, watch over him as we come together.

Gradually, I begin to liberate him of his clothes. I've seen him in so many astonishing outfits today, but there's genuinely nothing quite like the breathtaking sight of him naked.

We kiss and smile and caress as each item slowly gets tossed to the floor. I run my hands all over his body. I know it so well already, but I still feel like I'm mapping it all out, committing it to memory.

When he rolls over and drags me on top of him, I know what he's asking for, what he needs. So I reach for the lube—this one a warm, sensual cinnamon—and squirt some into each of our hands. He wraps his around both our lengths, pleasuring us together. I reach around and start to stretch myself, easing my fingers inside so I'm ready to take his cock.

Our kisses are slow and tender, mixed with panting breaths and moans. We watch each other through our eyelashes in the dimming light of the day. Fuck, I feel so lucky to be with him here like this.

I can fight it as much as I want by telling myself it's too fast. But I'm sure I'm falling in love. My heart aches so much for him.

It's amazing to me that we're hardly speaking, and yet our minds and bodies are so in sync. I fumble for a condom, and he allows me to roll it on him before I shift forward and angle him so his tip is resting against my entrance. It's been a fair while since I bottomed, but as he slowly pushes his way past my tight ring, I already know it's going to feel amazing.

"Yes, baby," I mumble against his lips as I lower myself down, taking him all the way inside me. Even with the condom, he feels so good—hot and hard and throbbing within me.

He clings to my side and rubs our cheeks together, gripping the back of my head. "Oscar," he groans. "Oscar, yes. Oh my god."

We rock slowly to start with, reveling in our intimate connection. His cock is long and slim like the rest of him, so it easily reaches my prostate, sending sparks flashing before my eyes with every thrust. Before long, our rhythm picks up speed naturally, and I start riding him with gusto. His kisses are almost desperate, and I crash my lips against him again and again.

"Yes, beautiful," I cry, slamming him into the mattress. "Mine, all mine."

"Yours," he grunts, digging his nails into my back. "Oh, Oscar, *oh.*"

I take myself in hand as my climax starts to build. I love that he's marking me, claiming me as his own. I can't blemish his perfect skin when he's got a pool party to attend tonight, but I can still declare that he's mine in a less permanent way. I drop my head back but manage to keep my eyes on him as I start coming with a roar, painting him with my seed. He looks so fucking gorgeous as my cream splatters all over his chest.

He whimpers and gnashes his teeth as a few moments later, he loses himself to his climax as well. I feel him pulsing inside me as he fills the condom, and I continue to impale myself on his cock, milking the very last drops of pleasure from him.

Then I lean down on trembling arms and kiss him with what little energy I have left. "My beautiful baby," I rasp against his lips.

"Oscar," he says reverently, stroking my back and sides where he's been scratching.

I just want to stay in this moment forever.

Even though I know we can't.

19

MALYK

The next couple of days go by far too fast. Wednesday, we wake up to a dozen easels set up on the lawn, and the art sessions go on all day. There's a break from the partying on Thursday when Emmalina organizes a small fleet of monster four-by-fours to take us out into the wilderness for a daytime hike that I thoroughly enjoy. The views are spectacular, and it feels so good to stretch my legs after several days cooped up indoors.

Don't get me wrong, I love a shagfest as much as the next guy. But it's not the same kind of cardio as trekking it up the side of a small mountain. The best part, though, is seeing Samson go nuts. He has to run and smell every single twig and rock and pee on everything, the whole while wagging his tail like a helicopter. When he runs back to greet us, he always gives us a big, toothy grin, like this is the best place on earth.

No, I take it back. All that's great, for sure. But the *best* thing is getting to hold Oscar's hand for the entire walk.

I'm smitten. It's hopeless. But I just feel so bloody amazing when he's near me, and knowing that I'm flying home on Sunday is making me want to soak up every moment I can with him like a plant drinking in sunshine before autumn comes. Or 'fall,' as Americans call it. I want to learn all his different words and see the world through different, older eyes. I know there's going to be so much distance between us, but my stupid heart is praying we can keep some kind of connection going.

That's in the future, though. In the present, we have a barbecue on Thursday night that's a lot more chilled than the other big party nights. There's no dress code for this event, even though most people still look pretty made up.

I've met a lot of the team from the Haus of Emmalina as well as other models, agents, photographers, and the rest. I honestly don't know if it's doing me any good or if it will lead anywhere, but it's certainly making me feel like this is a community in which I belong.

I know in the real world it won't be non-stop partying. In fact, that's a relief. I'll be thankful to take a break when I get home. But the buzz in the air when Emmalina brings out something from the upcoming collections for us to play with reminds me that what we do changes people's lives. Sure—it's not curing cancer. But people wear clothes *every single day.* Clothes can make a person feel incredible. Emmalina and her team design them, but I want to be part of the team that brings them to life.

I just hope this trip was worth it for that. If I can't keep Oscar, maybe I can start a new phase of my career.

It's what I've wanted for so long. I mean, I'd rather keep the man I'm falling in love with. But I just don't see how that can happen. My life and work are in London, his are in New York. It's not like I really love London especially, but it's where the opportunities are. And I'm just a few hours away from Mum.

Yeah, you've caught me. I've definitely lain awake a few nights wondering if I could uproot my whole life and relocate to America. But that's crazy. I can't leave everything I've worked for just because a couple of weeks ago I met a man who makes me feel…

Oh, god. He makes me feel like the center of the universe. Like the reason he exists. And the sex? Dear lord, the sex is out of this world. It's frankly outrageous how good he can make me feel.

But it's a fairy tale, and it will have to come to an end sooner or later. If I'm very lucky, though, my trajectory in the fashion industry is only just getting started. It's cold comfort, but comfort all the same.

I try my very best not to be mopey or sad on our last full day at Honeyrock. We have a late start, sleeping in before going to brunch, then taking Emmalina's limo back into the city to collect my suit. It seems a bit silly to make the journey again when we'll be traveling back to Oscar's the next day as well, but apparently, Briceson wouldn't hear of couriering my outfit over without seeing it on me first and checking it was absolutely perfect.

The store isn't on private hire today but it's still pretty quiet as Oscar and I enter hand in hand. Briceson gives us his full attention as he fusses over my final fitting. The purple suit looks as incredible as I remember it, but even better now that Briceson has made all his little tweaks.

"Gurl," he drawls with a couple of snaps of his fingers. "You're gonna bring the house down. Okay, let's get you out of this before you wrinkle it, then all your accessories are in this bag." He indicates a large square carrier on a nearby seat that's got the company's gold logo on it and soft pink tissue paper spilling out the top. "I threw a couple of extras in there," he tells me with a wink.

I wonder what he means, but he doesn't give me a chance to look before he whisks the bag away and leaves me to get changed again. I take my time, ensuring that I hang the suit up properly and don't crease it.

By the time I exit the little changing room Briceson is talking in hushed tones with Oscar, who looks kind of flustered, but when he sees me, he immediately smiles. "All good?"

"Yeah," I say as I look between them. "Great. What's going on here?"

"Nothing," says Briceson with a shrug.

He saunters over to me and takes the clothes hanger from me on two fingers, then spins around to face his employee who has materialized from nowhere. He's holding another suit bag, which I assume is my powder blue one. Briceson looks back at me.

"You're all paid up, and Charles here will make sure everything is packed properly in your car." He winks. "Go knock 'em dead, tiger."

"What was that about?" I ask Oscar a few minutes later as soon as we get into the limo.

He rubs the back of his neck and laughs ruefully. "He's given us a few extra things."

"Oh," I say with a frown. "Yeah, he showed me the bag. I hope they weren't too expensive."

Oscar shakes his head, then finally smiles as he takes my hand. "Emmalina actually covered the extras. I think she and Briceson have been in cahoots."

He grins, and so do I. I'm not sure how I feel about Emmalina buying me anything, but hopefully, it's nothing too big. And Oscar seems okay now, so I'm sure everything's fine.

We spend the drive back to the house discussing the people we've met this week. Oscar's been subtly letting me know whose social medias are worth following or whose emails I should note down. Amid all the whirlwind romance, I do feel like I've been networking the hell out of this thing.

Back home in London, it's not like people are *un*friendly, but I can't say I'm particularly close with anyone. Except maybe Jamie. We only just met, and most of our friendship has been via Instagram DMs, but a bit like Oscar, I do already feel a strong connection with him. But other than that, I realize just how lonely I've been since Chris and I broke up.

It's not like I haven't been trying to make friends and contacts in the business. But it's felt like Chris has been there every step of the way to thwart me like some kind of comic book villain. Even here, he's tried his best, but Oscar has protected me like the white knight he claims not to be.

I guess what I'm trying to put into words as we approach Honeyrock again is that I feel like I'm already building a much better network here, stateside.

And then I'm going to have to walk away from it all.

No, I refuse to dwell on the negatives. There have been so many unbelievable positives this week, and this is the grand finale. No matter what happens I know that my life has changed for the better because of this incredible opportunity. I won't waste any of the chances I've been given.

Especially not when it comes to my final night on holiday with Oscar.

I know it will be different tomorrow. We'll be driving back to his place, and then I have to get up early for my flight home. So tonight is the big send-off, and I intend on looking sensational.

Samson joins us as we're getting ready. To begin with, he's excited by all the movement, but soon enough he settles down on the bed to watch his daddy and me get ready. I'm glad for the calmer atmosphere as for some inexplicable reason I'm nervous. I know my outfit is stunning and that I've already done a good job making an impression on people this week. But this is the last they'll see of me, I guess. I want to dazzle beyond a doubt.

The ensemble doesn't take all that long to put on, but I then take my time focusing on my hair and make-up. I've kept it quite casual this week, but I feel like this is the time for a full face and all the products. Like I'm a debutant doing everything she can to catch the eye of the man she loves in one of those Regency dramas.

There I go again, still worrying about impressing Oscar. I'm pretty sure he doesn't need any help fancying me, but I just want to knock his socks off. I want to make him speechless.

I'm so preoccupied that I don't realize when he takes a suit bag into the bathroom. One of the staff brought our purchases up from the car, so I've kind of lost track of what is what.

But I'm about to find out what 'extras' Briceson snuck in for us.

"What do you think?" a nervous voice asks just as I'm putting the final touches on my lips. I adjust my gaze to look at Oscar in the reflection of the mirror… and my jaw drops.

The old jeans are gone. As is the usual button down and slightly scuffed gray loafers. There's definitely no ancient baseball cap.

Instead, he's wearing a matching jacket and trousers made from a grayish-blue material with a fine checkered pattern of tan lines mixed with a lighter blue. His waist-coat—or vest as the Americans call it—is also a rich tan, as are his leather shoes. A crisp white shirt is buttoned up all the way, and his tie looks like it's almost made out of denim. The ensemble is finished off with a tan pocket handkerchief with cream polka dots, a stunning blue stone ring on his pinky, and his own fancy watch I've only seen in its box until now. His beard even looks like it's been neatly oiled and groomed.

"Fuck," I manage to croak eventually, rising to my

feet as if in a trance. "Is this what you and Briceson were fighting about? I *knew* something sneaky was going on! Cheese on toast, I need to send him a bouquet of bloody roses. Oh! *This* is what Emmalina insisted on buying?"

Oscar nods and smiles shyly as I reach him, glancing at me through his eyelashes. "It's a bit fancier than my usual garb," he says, stating the bloody obvious. "But I take it that's a 'yes' to liking it."

"Too damn right," I say, running the tie through my hand. It's not actually denim, I realize up close, but a clever blue with a tiny light dot print. It's soft and smooth against my palm as I slide it out from underneath the waistcoat.

"Hey," Oscar protests with a crooked eyebrow.

I grin devilishly. "Wotcha gonna do about it, old man?"

He growls and yanks my hips so they slam against his. Blood rushes to my cock, even though I know we really shouldn't do anything naughty right now when we've spent so long getting pretty.

He leans his face into mine so we're nearly kissing. But I think he sees my lippy and gloss and decides on a different approach, which is to attack my neck with kisses and grab my crotch to massage it. I respond by seizing his arse, getting two really good handfuls to knead. I gasp as he threatens to give me a hickey, but I can't make myself pull away.

Luckily, there's someone sensible in the room, and he's also the most gorgeous. Samson barks loudly and jumps up from where he was lying on the bed, breaking us from our lusty haze. I laugh as we step apart and look at our best boy wagging his tail like this is the funnest game ever.

"Good puppy," I say, fussing the top of his head.

Oscar fusses me at the same time. He straightens my scarf and brushes against my neck where he was kissing, presumably so it's not wet with spit. Normally I'd be totally fine with that—hell, I want the damn love bite—but not tonight. I don't want anyone to have the excuse to judge me about anything if I can help it.

"Oh, Briceson also got us these," Oscar says. He reaches into the bag that had my scarf and shoebox in it. Everything was mixed in with the pink paper, so I missed another package. But Oscar carefully unwraps it for us now.

In all the excitement of finding a suit, I'd completely forgotten that this was a masquerade ball. He pulls out two fascinating pieces. They're half masks on sticks, so more for posing with than actually wearing. But they're kind of made up of squares in a geometric pattern— almost like a large pixelation of a classic Venetian mask. They could be naff but I think they look modern and sleek. He hands me the black one, and he keeps the gold.

"Are you ready?" he asks in a sultry voice as he holds it up.

I'm about to say 'hell yeah!' but I pause. I want to preserve this moment a little longer while it's just the two of us. Well...the three of us. Samson's still wagging his tail happily, waiting for our next move.

I look back at the man I've fallen so hard for, loving

how fucking hot he is in this moment with his dapper threads. But it's more than just about aesthetics. We're sharing something special together.

"Can I take your photo?" I blurt out.

His eyebrows rise. "Me?"

I nod, certain of this idea now. "Yeah. You're bloody stunning. I probably won't do a fraction of a good job compared to you, but I'd like to try." I get my phone out and wiggle it at him. I might not be a professional, but I've managed to keep my Instagram in order up until this point. I reckon I could snap a decent pic or two.

I know how to get some natural light on him, so I get him to stand in front of the window and pose a little. He keeps laughing self-consciously, but I think that just adds to the charm of it all. After a while, though, I think I've got what I wanted, and now I'm after something else.

"Take some selfies with me?" I ask quietly. "Not for the Gram. Just for me."

He bites his lip, then comes over to hug me tenderly. "I'd love that," he murmurs into my ear.

We take a lot more of these. We both look into the camera for a while, then he starts nuzzling my neck and making me laugh as I keep on snapping. Samson pushes between us and makes us both yelp as we try not to get his delightful slobber on our couture. But then we kneel on the floor so our heads are all lined up, and I take a bunch more snaps.

I get pictures taken of me for a living. I know I'm photogenic. But without even looking at these, I know they're going to be something I'll treasure for a long time.

I'm stocking up a collection of keepsakes from Oscar to take with me back to London when my heart breaks into a thousand pieces. But for now, I'm full of love as we head down to the ball, and I'm feeling like a real fairy-tale princess.

Who knows? I might still get my happily ever after. I don't really see how, but for this night, I wish upon my lucky star and keep the hope alive.

20

MALYK

We're not late, but we're certainly not the first ones to arrive at the final event of the retreat. I try to keep calm and not smile too much as I sense the heads turning to look at us, but it's hard not to feel proud. I know Briceson did an amazing job with my suit, but I'm actually beaming for Oscar in this moment. He looks like a million bucks, and I'm so proud to have him on my arm. Even Samson has a fancy bow tie on his collar and looks adorable.

"My, my, my," Emmalina says as she comes sauntering over to us. She's got an enormous feather fan in her hand that she's gently wafting against her bosom. People naturally part for her as she cuts across the dance floor because her dress is so huge. It's a delicate pink and covered in about a thousand crystals that glint in the light. "Look at you two," she says with a wink as she arrives in front of us. "I take it you had fun with Bricey."

"It was incredible," I tell her sincerely. "Thank you so much for the opportunity. I can't tell you how much I appreciate it."

She waves her fan and shakes her head. "I should be thanking *you*. The way you're wearing that thing… *Damn*, child. It's an honor to have you here tonight."

For a second, I don't know what to say. *She's thanking me?* What kind of parallel universe is this?

"It-it's my pleasure," I manage to stutter.

She smiles knowingly before nodding once at Oscar, then wandering off to greet more guests.

"See," Oscar says, only sounding slightly smug. "I told you you'd made an impression."

I cling to his arm, even though I'm taller than him in these heels. "I know, but…" I say weakly as we make our way to the trays of Champagne saucers.

"Seeing is believing?" Oscar suggests.

I just smile, and we toast our glasses with a little clink.

"To new horizons," he says meaningfully.

"To new friends," I say with just as much sincerity.

Samson barks and chases his tail in a circle, making not only us but everyone around us laugh.

"I think he agrees with you," Oscar says as we head out into the garden. "To new friends." We tap our glasses together, and I hope he knows that I mean him.

The pool no longer looks like a man-made structure but rather some tropical lagoon that's sprung up in New York. The surface is covered with artificial lily pads and several kinds of floating LED-lit flowers. Under the surface is illuminated as well, and I can see cute little mechanical fish whizzing around.

On the patio, there are now several huge, lush shrubs that make the house suddenly feel like it's in a jungle. The flamingos are back, but there are also people who I assume are trained professionals with gorgeous tropical birds resting on leather gauntlets the carers are wearing on their arms. A steel band is playing, and there's a scent of mango and other juicy fruits in the air.

"Wow," I say. "Every time I think Emmalina has outdone herself, she proves me wrong."

Oscar chuckles. "I know, right? Come on. Let's mingle."

We spend some time chatting with guests and eating canapés. But then the steel band swaps out for a string quartet and the mood shifts. Oscar gently guides me away from the people we were just talking to, holds up his mask, and peeks at me through it.

"Can this stranger have a dance?"

I giggle. I'm not normally one to giggle. But it bubbles out of me as I lift my own mask.

"You may," I tell him and hold my other hand out, fingertips slightly curled so he can take them. He does so and kisses my knuckles before we both place our masks down on a nearby table, then he leads me to the dance floor.

He holds one of my hands and wraps the other around my waist. I mimic him and rest my temple against his, breathing in his cologne and feeling his heartbeat through his chest. It's magical. A perfect night to end a perfect week.

A lump threatens to rise in my throat, but I make myself swallow it down. It's easier to forget my worries when I see Samson parading around the guests with some kind of cream on his nose. I don't know what he's stuck his face in, but I chuckle and figure maybe it's best not to find out.

"I love your laugh," Oscar comments, making my heart ache.

"I love…" I begin to say. *You* is how I want to finish the sentence. Our time is coming to an end, and I have to tell him. No matter what happens when I go home, I want him to know.

But the word dies in my throat. Chris is staring daggers at me from across the patio. When I lock eyes with him, he gives me a subtle point, then gestures to himself with his eyebrows raised. He wants a word, and he's not amused.

Part of me wants to blow him off. He's almost certainly just trying to mess with me as I dance with Oscar. But then I remind myself that he is still technically my agent, and it might be important. He could have been trying to tell me something for days and is pissed off because I've either been avoiding him or hidden away with Oscar.

Whatever it is, I decide to get it over and done with now so that he'll intrude on as little of our evening as possible. I squeeze Oscar's hip and give him a tight smile. "Would you excuse me a minute? I need to see what Chris wants. I'll be right back."

Oscar glances over. Chris gives him a smile that doesn't reach his eyes and a small wave, but we all know he's just being polite. When I think of how he sucked up to Oscar to start with and now he can barely contain his contempt…I'd roll my eyes, but I figure one of us two needs to remain professional, and I'm happy for it to be me.

But before I can walk over, Oscar squeezes my hip back and leans in to kiss my cheek. "I'll be *right* here," he growls as if he can warn Chris through me not to fuck around because he'll be watching us. I don't care that Chris can't hear the mild threat. It warms my heart all the same.

With one last hug, I finally let Oscar go and strut over to Chris, eating up the dance floor like it's my own personal runway. *Yeah, bitch,* I think toward Chris as several people turn their heads to look. *I belong here, whether you like it or not.*

Chris isn't backing down, though. His face looks reasonably calm, but as I approach, I can see the telltale vein throbbing in his temple that means he's furious. "Well, that sounds like a 'you' problem," I mutter to myself as I weave around some guests.

I'm not going to let him intimidate me.

"Hi," I say pleasantly as I approach him, but then it's like I can't stop my mouth from moving. "Where's Frans?"

I look around because I'd genuinely like to say hello, but from the way Chris's mouth thins, I know I've put my foot in it. That's what happens when you bring eye candy to try and make someone jealous, then ignore them, though. I hope Frans is off somewhere, being very busy and important. Who knows? Maybe he's struck a deal with one of the agents here. I hope so.

"I see you've decided to play this game until the end," Chris says smoothly, but there's an icy edge to his words.

"What game?" I reply just as frostily.

"Does Wainwright know you're using him to get ahead?" he asks. I try to keep my cool, but his words nettle me.

"I'm not using anyone," I say evenly. I manage to keep a smile on my lips, but the rage in my eyes is probably quite obvious.

He shrugs innocently. "You tried to use me to get here. What am I supposed to think?"

I swallow and count to three before calmly responding. It's time to put this to bed now. "I dated you because once upon a time, I thought you were charming and sweet. You were the one who promised to bring me here, then laughed at me in front of a whole shoot when I realized you never meant a word of it—about the trip or our relationship."

"Dating?" he scoffs as his eyebrows shoot up. "Now that's delusional. And I might have *talked* about Honey-rock, but if you thought that meant an invite, I'm sorry, mate, but that's on you."

I fold my arms and look him up and down. "Gaslighting me now, are we? You really are a charmer. If that's all, I've left my date alone and really need to be getting back to him."

"Oh yes, the date you preferred to spend this whole

week with rather than actually working. We've all noticed."

I finally give in and roll my eyes. "Which is it, Chris?" I ask scathingly. "Am I faking it with Oscar, or are we shagging like rabbits? Make up your mind."

"I don't have to," he says smoothly. "I just know what it looks like. Unprofessional."

I shake my head. "If that's what you think, whatever. I know how hard I've worked this week. I don't need to prove anything to you."

I only feel a twinge of guilt as I say that. In my mind, I know I could have maybe done more socializing. But Oscar assured me time and again that I'd done enough, and I didn't need to overwhelm Emmalina or anyone else. There is such a thing as being *too* keen.

But Chris's smirk makes my stomach drop. "Actually, you did have something to prove to me, and you failed."

"Failed?" I repeat incredulously, trying not to show my apprehension.

"You came up short," he rephrases like I'm an idiot. "It's my professional opinion that you're not a good fit with the McKay's Models brand, and I've requested that you be dropped from our books, effective immediately." He gives me a savage smile. "I think you've damaged our reputation more than enough. And it's not like you've exactly been jam-packed with shoots, now has it?"

The room spins, and for a second, I think I'm going to pass out. But there Oscar is, immediately by my side, catching me before I can fall.

I wish he wasn't there, though. As much as I don't want to crash to the ground, I absolutely don't want him to witness this humiliation. It seems there's no stopping it, though.

"What's going on?" he demands.

People are starting to turn and look, and for the first time tonight, I wish with all my heart they weren't. Even Samson comes trotting over to us, bless him. He whimpers and sits by my feet, looking up at us with his big black eyes.

Chris, on the other hand, seems to be reveling in the attention. Basking in it, almost.

"Oh," he says nonchalantly to Oscar. "I was just informing Mr. Defries here that he's no longer a good fit for McKay's Models and that we'll no longer be representing him."

"Well, that's ridiculous," Oscar says with a frown. "On what grounds? You know what? Never mind. I'll call Marcus myself and ask."

"Oscar, no," I hiss in mortification. I'm pretty sure Mr. McKay doesn't know I exist. I don't want him to find out about all this petty drama.

"He's right," Chris says smugly, jutting his chin at me. "I'm his agent, so I get the final say. You're not pulling in any favors this time, I'm afraid."

"We'll see about that," Oscar snaps. Samson barks, and the people around us are murmuring. Hot tears prick at my eyes, and the only reason I'm not bawling is that I wouldn't give Chris the satisfaction. At least Emmalina isn't here to witness any of my disgrace.

I thought the lowest Chris would go would be to try

and keep me from getting work. I never thought that he'd have the power to drop me or that he'd even stoop so low.

I've been the world's biggest fool.

"Thank you for the opportunity," is all I can manage to say to my ex-boyfriend and now ex-agent as well. My voice is trembling as I struggle to hold back the tears. "I appreciate your time."

Chris laughs at me. Of course he does. "You're very welcome, Mr. Defries," he says jovially. "Good luck in your next endeavors."

Before he can humiliate me any further, I turn on my heels and start walking, not daring to look up at anyone as I make a beeline for the house. I feel rather than see Oscar and Samson next to me. Oscar knows better than to try and talk to me in this moment, so he just follows as I hurry upstairs.

I fumble for my key, letting us into our room. To think, just a couple of hours ago, we were on cloud nine, getting ready here.

Now everything's fallen apart.

Well, I remember what I thought about Chris and Honeyrock before when this whole mess started.

You can't lose what you never had.

Oscar was never going to be mine to keep. And my career has been crushed before it even really got a chance to start.

It's no surprise that once the door is locked, I tumble onto the bed in all my fancy clothes and burst into tears. I feel like my soul is trying to claw out from my body. When Oscar and Samson lie on the bed beside me, I just cry harder.

"You'll mess up your suit," I manage to protest as Oscar wraps his arms around me.

"I don't care," Oscar says quietly.

He holds me until I cry myself to sleep.

21

OSCAR

"I don't understand how this can be the end," I say. I know I'm repeating myself, but I can't help it. "Just like that?"

It's early the next morning, and Malyk is packing his bags with a cold, detached determination that I don't like. It's as if he's turned into a robot.

"If Chris doesn't want to represent me anymore, then that *is* it," he says again. But this time, at least, he elaborates. "And yeah, another agent could take me on, but why would they want to? My work record is so patchy, no one's going to want to touch me. And I can't go running around telling everyone that it's Chris's fault as well. I'll get a reputation as a troublemaker that will go far beyond McKay's. If I want to get representation in London, I'll just have to start from scratch and hope someone takes a chance on me. But that's not going to get many bills paid in the meantime."

The mention of money makes me feel sick. I'd never let him fall on hard times. Never. But he was so resistant to me taking care of him this week. If he was uncomfortable with me picking up the check for dinner, how would he ever be okay with me offering to pay his rent? Would he accept any kind of financial help from me, or would that twist our relationship into something approaching a business agreement in his mind?

But I'm sure there's even more going on under the surface than he's letting on. Sometimes he gets a genuine fear in his eyes when we discuss finances. I have a strong feeling that he's gotten himself into some kind of trouble. It's not uncommon. A lot of models and influencers do it in an attempt to keep up with an ever-changing industry.

The thought of him going hungry or, god forbid, ending up on the streets, makes me want to vomit.

Yet he's folding socks with such an outwardly calm demeanor you'd think he was talking about the weather.

I glance down at Samson, who's unusually subdued as well, then tug at my hair. "But you're...Malyk, you're fucking *stunning*. McKay would be an absolute fool to let you go, never mind thinking you'll struggle to get representation anywhere else. If you'd just let me call him—"

"No," he interrupts loudly. His beautiful gray-green eyes blaze at me. "Don't get involved. I mean it. I can't get a reputation as some brat who pulls strings to get his own way either."

"That's not what this is at all," I protest. "Oakley is lying and abusing his power. If anyone should get fired, it's him! We can't take this lying down, baby."

I know I should probably be packing as well,

because at this rate, he's going to be all done and then storm off and leave me behind. But this isn't how I imagined leaving this room where we fell in love at all. I know neither of us has admitted those words out loud, but I'm certain it's true in my heart. That's how I feel, at the very least.

He shrugs and closes up one of his bags. "It is what it is. I'm not giving up. I'm just accepting reality."

"Well, I don't like reality," I cry, throwing my hands in the air.

He pauses, and for the first time since we woke up, I see his steely veneer crack. "Neither do I," he whispers, staring at the bed covers. "But I can't do anything to change it other than fight on my terms and not give up."

"Exactly," I say, moving around the bed and wrapping my hand around his arm. "You can't let Oakley win."

The walls come back up. *Shit.*

"He already has," Malyk says as he pulls away from me and hauls the suitcase off the bed. "At least in terms of McKay's. And I'm sure Emmalina won't want to touch me now." He blinks as he looks around the room and then out the window. "I just hope this week wasn't a total loss and that I still have some friends in this industry."

I shake my head and squeeze his arm, encouraging him to look my way. "You've got *me,*" I say fiercely.

His smile is so sad it breaks my heart in two. "I do," he says softly. "But you'll be in New York. A little far away for comforting hugs."

I pull him against me now and throw my arms around him, pressing my face against his neck. He clings to me like a life raft. "Don't go," I rasp, finally caving in and asking the impossible. The ridiculous. "Stay with me."

"I can't," he says. I don't ask why. I know it's insane to even ask. But I want him to do it anyway.

"You've got nothing to lose. You could start over."

He bites his lip. "I've been looking up US immigration policies," he admits with a shaky laugh as tears spill down his face. "You know. For reasons. It's really, really hard without getting sponsored by work or marriage, but they are *crazy* hot on green card fraud. I could maybe try and get some kind of holiday visa, but even then…" He trails off and shakes his head. "I just have to go home for now. Maybe when things settle down, I can revisit my options."

"Of course," I say, regretting asking. I should have known it wasn't just a case of uprooting his life. The visa thing never occurred to me, and I feel like an idiot. I'm the one who should be taking care of him, and yet I can't work out how to fix this problem.

I desperately want to talk to McKay. He is my friend. It wouldn't be out of line. But Malyk is so fierce in his insistence that I don't. I'm sure it'll be the same with Emmalina. Perhaps once the dust is settled, he'll think differently.

God, everything about this sucks. For a while, I just hold him, so grateful that he lets me. But then he pulls away with a sigh and looks around the room.

"I'd like to go before the house gets busy."

I nod. "Of course." The party went on late last night, so I imagine most people will sleep in. Linny gives people the whole day to depart. But I have to agree that right now, I just want to get Malyk home where we can be alone, and I can give him all the love I've got.

It doesn't take me very long to get my shit together. What slows me down is Samson's whimpering and constant headbutting against my legs. "I know, buddy," I grumble at him. "But we have to go home now, okay?"

He lies down by the foot of the bed and pouts until we finally all head out the door.

Malyk doesn't look back as we make our way through the house out to the car I've organized. But I take a moment to absorb this place that I've been coming to for over a decade. With all my thoughts of quitting fashion photography recently, I wondered if this would be my last year.

It's like I'm seeing it with new eyes and that should have been a good thing. This place should be filled with memories of Malyk, and it is. However, they're tinged with sadness and anger and regret. I assumed we'd be back next year, but now I have no idea what will happen.

Perhaps it was my last Honeyrock, after all.

The journey back into the city couldn't feel more different from the one we took yesterday. We don't talk, and the driver has the good sense to leave us alone. Malyk clings to me like a barnacle and stares at the partition wall for the entire drive. I don't break the silence out of respect for his feelings but also because I think I've run out of things I can say.

I'm just so angry at the universe for the way things have turned out. If I wanted to sucker punch Oakley before, you can bet your bottom dollar that now I'd happily drop-kick him off the top of the Empire State Building. What a douchebag. I mean it that he shouldn't be allowed to continue to work at McKay's agency. Who knows what other young men he's screwing over—in the bedroom and in the workplace.

But as much as I'd like to protect those hypothetical guys, Malyk is all I really care about right now. I'd do anything to make his pain go away. The fact that he allows me to carry a couple of his bags into my building as well as my own speaks volumes.

When he lies down on my couch with Samson, I cover him with a blanket. When I make him some hot, buttery ramen, he says a genuine thanks, but he struggles to eat more than a few bites.

In the end, I wordlessly take him by the hand and lead him into my bedroom. We don't speak, but when I raise my eyebrows at him, he nods before cupping my face and kissing me tenderly on the mouth.

Our lovemaking is gentle and sensual. When he comes wrapped in my arms with me buried inside him, he starts to cry again. I let him.

I shower him. I tuck him into bed. And when morning comes after a sleepless night, I go with him to the airport and stay with him all the way until the security gate. His bags are gone. It's just us left, standing by the stream of people that he has to join imminently. I hold him until the last possible moment.

"I love you," I say when the time comes.

He kisses me with lips salty from silent tears. "I love you, too," he replies. It's so un-ceremonial. So anticlimactic. But I know with my whole heart it's the truth, and I'm glad we spoke the words out loud, even if now it's not going to do much good. I'll carry them in my soul, though.

And then that's it. I watch him walk away until he vanishes from sight. But it takes me several minutes to make my feet move so I can head home.

Because I know once I get there, I'll have to start living the rest of my life.

And I have no fucking clue how I'm going to do that.

22

———

MALYK

Well, nothing's official yet, but no one's talking to me either. I tried calling Rose, one of the secretaries in the London office, but all she could tell me was that Chris is apparently still in America and she didn't have any messages for me. I didn't want to outright ask 'have I been fired?' so I had to leave it at that.

Therefore, I'm back here in my cramped room in a house I share with strangers, with nothing to do and no one to turn to. My two stunning suits hang outside my wardrobe doors in their bags. I can't bear to look at them. Their presence here just adds insult to injury. They don't belong in this crappy place.

Neither do I. Not that it's going to be an issue for much longer, I imagine. I should be fine to pay this month's rent, but what about next month? I need to get a job in a shop or something so I can give myself a little breathing room.

I've still got my Insta, I guess, so I'm not completely cut off. But I don't have enough followers to even be considered for the bonus scheme, and even then, I'm sure you have to be in the US to be able to apply, which is frankly ironic at this point. I can totally still do paid partnerships, but I haven't talked to any suppliers for a while since I've been with McKay's, and to get that back up and running will take energy I just don't have right now.

Jetlag is still messing with me, and I keep falling asleep at odd times, then waking up feeling rotten. I've been lying on my bed post nap for a while, feeling sorry for myself and trying my best not to think about Oscar. But it's pretty impossible. I texted to let him know I got home safe, and he responded with a message saying that he loved me and missed me already. I so want to text him all the time, but I think that's just going to make things harder in the long run, so I've resisted so far.

A walk might do me good. If nothing else, it'll get some fresh air in my lungs and stretch my legs. Not allowing myself time to talk my way out of it, I groan and sit up to force my feet into my trainers.

It's mid-afternoon, so in between lunchtime and rush hour, but it's London so it's still pretty bustling. I have an idea to walk down to the little newsagents, but I don't want to spend any money, even if it's just a quid for a chocolate bar. I head that way anyway, if only to give my feet a direction to point in.

I feel like a boat lost at sea. I've got an anchor to throw out but nothing to hook it on. God, a week ago, it seemed like my world was full of possibilities. Now I have no idea what I'm supposed to do.

Find another agency, I suppose. McKay's isn't the

only one in town. But I loved how inclusive it is. I guess that doesn't matter anymore. I still wasn't a right fit for them.

I don't belong anywhere, it seems.

I shove my hands into my pockets and take some deep breaths. This might feel like the end of the world, but it isn't. I'm still here. I'm still fighting.

Maybe when I pick myself up again, I'll feel strong enough to contact Oscar. That thought cheers me up a fraction. It's not like I have a plan or anything, but just promising myself that this isn't really the end helps a little.

There's still hope.

It's also hard not to let my anger toward Chris overwhelm me. Why did he have to be so mean? So petty? He didn't want me, but that meant no one else could have me either? That makes no sense. Well, I guess it does to him if his goal is to spread misery in this world. I'd rather spread joy, but that's me.

The one good thing out of this whole mess, I suppose, is that I don't have to see Chris anytime soon —or ever again, maybe. In a way, he's set me free. He no longer has any power over me unless I give it to him. Which is why I have to let this rage go. He might have gotten the last word in at McKay's, but this is my life, and I'm not giving any more energy to him.

"That's it," I say out loud to myself as I trudge down the street toward the bus stop that's just before the shop. "Fresh starts right now. Positive thinking only."

I start making a plan to head home and work on my Insta content. I've got a bunch of footage I can be using to work the algorithms without giving away any details of where I've been this week or who I was with. I've also got some of my old contacts at a couple of online fashion outlets that I could hit up and see if they want me to do any promo. In my room, that felt impossible, but I'm sure they'd still be up for hearing from me, and it's lucrative if I put my mind to it and do it right. Quick paychecks are going to be essential now unless I want to resort to doing something on one of those private apps I'll regret.

There we go. Having *some* kind of direction makes me feel like I can breathe a little better again. All is not lost just yet.

The bus pulls up to the stop, and an older lady gets off with a shopping trolley bag, drawing my attention that way.

I do a double take.

I stop walking.

"Oh my fucking *god!*" I shriek as tears spring into my eyes.

The little old lady pauses and looks at me in surprise as the bus pulls back out into the traffic. "Are you quite all right, dear?" she asks kindly.

I lift a trembling hand and point at the side of the bus stop. "That's me," I whisper.

She adjusts her headscarf before turning to look at the poster I'm pointing at. It's honestly taller than me, which is saying something. Then her face splits into a wide grin. "Goodness gracious, so it is! Don't you look beautiful? What a stunning photo."

"My boyfriend took it," I say without thinking as a

tear slips down my cheek.

It's the one he showed me the day of the shoot. The one I'd be happy to use on my epitaph. How fitting, when it feels for the past couple of days like I was disappearing from the world, now there it is.

I'm not sure if it feels like a gravestone or a rebirth, though.

I drag my eyes away from it to see the lady beaming at me. "Well, then. What is it my grandkids say these days? Sounds like couple goals. You have a lovely day now, darling."

"Thank you," I manage to mumble. She totters off with her shopping trolley, and my gaze slips back toward the bus stop. I swallow, but there's a pretty big lump lodged in my throat.

My god, I look magnificent.

It's just me on this particular image. I guess there's a series, and there will be other posters in various places featuring some of the other models as well as group shots. But I'm sprawled on the edge of the fountain with my head tipped back as I give a sultry stare into the lens. The make-up I'm selling shimmers in the natural light. With all my fairy garb on, I do look kind of like a goddess.

Thoughts of Oscar overwhelm me, and it takes everything I have not to call him up right this instant. But as elated as I am to see my campaign out in the wild, the happiness is obviously mixed in with sorrow.

I'm not with the agency anymore. I should be texting Jamie to celebrate. I should be searching online to see who else I recognize in the final ads. But I'm not part of that company now, as far as I know. I suppose this might help me get a new agent, though. Having a national campaign to my name will go a long way to proving I actually *am* worthy of representation.

Yes. I'm going to cling to that positivity with my bloody fingernails. And I might not feel able to reach out to Oscar now, but I still pull out my phone and take some snaps of the poster. Then once I've wiped my face dry, I get some selfies in front of it as well. If things pick up and I feel better, I can message them to him later.

For now, I'll definitely put them on my Insta. Before that, though, I select my favorite couple of shots, then text them over to my mum.

Look, Mum! I'm on a bus stop! I write with several excitable emojis. She's at work, so I don't expect a reply back. But when I see the three dots moving, I hang on before closing my phone screen.

OMG YOU LOOK INCREDIBLE! She fires off immediately. Followed by: *I'm so proud of you, sweetheart. You're following your dreams. My little superstar.*

The tears well up in my eyes again. *I'm trying, Mum,* I think as I send her a simple heart to try and convey how much her words mean to me.

Who knows what the future might hold, but I'm not giving up yet.

And that includes my biggest dream of all that happens to live both on the other side of the Atlantic and also within my heart.

"I'm not giving up on us yet either, Oscar," I whisper to myself as I take one last look at the bus stop, then begin walking home.

23

OSCAR

"No, Samson. Not now."

There's a pause until I give in and crack one of my eyes open. He's sitting there, looking at me with his big ol' eyes, his tail thumping hopefully on the floor. I gave him a walk earlier, but I don't think that's what he's asking for now.

I'm fully aware of how pathetic I am. I'm lying on the couch with a blanket draped over me. There's an empty pizza box, a half-melted ice cream tub, and a couple of beer bottles littering my coffee table. I'm not watching a sad romantic movie, but I have got a ridiculous sci-fi on with lots of explosions to complete the look.

I'm a cliché, and I don't care.

Luckily, I don't have any work lined up for a while. I usually need a break after Honeyrock because Emmalina has tired me out. I never thought that this time I'd be nurturing a bruised and battered heart.

It's been a few days, and Malyk hasn't texted. I'm

making myself give him space. I know he's going through a lot. But it's so hard. I just want to swoop in and fix everything, even if I have no clue how. More than once, I've had to stop myself from looking up last-minute flights to London.

Today I cracked and finally stopped pretending to be okay. That young man stole my heart and took it back across the Atlantic with him. I miss him every minute, and I'm scared this is it. That he's going to vanish from my life, and I'll never see him again.

Samson whimpers and places his paw on my arm. I sigh and look at him again. "It's not like I *let* him leave, did I?" I protest.

He barks and bats his paw against my arm like I can just open a door and summon Malyk to me.

Having spent a little over a week in his company—and not just with him but *glued* to his side—it feels horribly weird to be alone again. Which is crazy. I've been on my own since Jerry moved out. I'm perfectly happy with my own company.

Yet here I am, the epitome of a sad dysfunctional loser, slowly becoming one with my couch.

The sound of my cell phone ringing makes me yelp, it startles me so much. In that moment, I'm kind of glad no one is here to witness my embarrassment. When I look at the caller ID and don't recognize it, I consider letting it go to voice mail. But I'm an adult and a professional, and it could be important.

There's a tiny part of me that hopes it's Malyk calling from a phone I don't know, and ultimately that's what gets me to pick up.

Oh, how wrong I am.

"Oscar Wainwright speaking," I say in a breezy tone that might convince whoever's on the other end of the line that I don't have pizza crumbs on my chest that I brush off as I sit up.

"Wainwright," the voice down the line says with barely concealed anger.

I blink down at Samson like he might have an explanation. But he's still, like he's listening in on the conversation with his superior doggy hearing. Then I realize I do, in fact, know the person disturbing my wallowing.

"Oakley?" I reply in confusion. "What can I do for you?"

"Oh," he scoffs. "I think you've done quite enough, don't you?"

I'm still confused. "You've lost me," I say as politely as I can. If anyone should be pissed in this conversation right now, it's me. *He* was the one who fucked Malyk over, not only potentially ruining his life but also pulling him out of mine.

In fact, my anger is starting to rise pretty quickly, so he better say his piece fast if he wants to get it out before I hang up the damn phone.

"What did you say to McKay?" he snarls. I think of how he sucked up to me on that photo shoot only a few weeks ago. Pathetic.

"I haven't spoken to Marcus since I left London," I say honestly.

He laughs. It's cold and loud, making me wince and pull the phone slightly away from my ear for a second.

"Don't try that bullshit with me, mate," he snaps. "I heard you with Defries. You were chomping at the bit to go running over there to plead your case to keep that lazy boy on the books. Well, congratulations. I guess you got your wish."

I stand up so fast I almost tangle my feet in the blanket and fall. Samson also jumps up, and his tail starts wagging again. "Malyk's not being dropped from the agency?" I splutter as I shake the blanket free.

Oakley huffs. "I honestly have no idea. I guess, maybe? I don't know because *I got fired,* and I'm calling to let you know that *I* know it's all your fucking fault. Ten years I spent working my way up there! And your meddling has undone it all! I'd ask if the sex was really worth it, but I know it's not."

I'm only half-listening to his rant. I tuned out after the part where he said he was fired. I'm gleeful because he deserves it, but that's actually not my concern right now. All I care about is Malyk.

"Look, buddy," I say in a forcefully cheerful tone. "I'm sorry you lost your job, but I honestly didn't have a single thing to do with it. Maybe if you hadn't tried to treat one of your own models so appallingly, this wouldn't have happened. But I can't say I'm sorry or surprised."

He splutters loudly down the line. "How dare you!" he yells. "I am nothing but a professional, and I'm *damn* good at my job."

"Then you shouldn't have any trouble finding a new one, should you, Mr. Oakley? Good night. I doubt our paths will cross again."

With an immense deal of satisfaction, I close the call and block his number.

Fired.

Fucking delicious.

I'm already scrolling through my contacts, looking for McKay's number. Malyk said I wasn't allowed to pull in any favors to try and protect him or get him back on the books, which I've respected. But he never said I couldn't call my friend up and ask if Malyk was *still* employed by the agency. I wouldn't be breaking his trust, and I'd also know that something about this horrible mess had been fixed.

But I pause just before hitting the call button.

If I didn't fill McKay in on the situation and get Oakley rightfully dismissed, then who did?

Of course I already know.

I continue scrolling through my contacts until I find the one I need. It only rings a couple of times until the call goes through.

"Oscar, darling!" Emmalina cries. The background noise sounds like she's at a party. "What can I do for you?"

"Um, have you got a second to talk?" I check.

She laughs good-naturedly. "We already are, sweetie. What's up?"

I exhale and massage the back of my neck, looking down at Samson. I'm scared to get my hopes up. "I was just wondering if you'd been in touch with Marcus McKay lately?"

Her soft laugh is very telling. "Oh, yes. We had a delightful chitchat over dinner last night. I felt he should be made aware of certain events that happened under my roof."

I lick my lips. I was stupid to think that just because she wasn't there to witness Oakley's scene herself that she wouldn't have heard all about it. But she didn't have to then *do* anything about it.

"Thank you," I say with utmost sincerity.

I hear her smirk down the line. "So? Did that little weasel get the boot?"

I laugh and rub my chin. "Oh, he sure did," I inform her. "He called me being all butt hurt over it. I was going to call McKay myself, but I don't know what the situation is with Malyk yet, and I wanted to get all the facts before I risk doing his career any more harm than it's already suffered."

There's a pause. "You've not talked to your little sugar plum yet?" she asks.

I bite my lip, worry crawling back into my chest. "No. We've barely even texted since he flew back home. I was trying to give him space, but—"

"Oh, for the love of…" Linny interrupts me. "Men! You're all useless. Close the damn call. It's not me you should be speaking to, you dummy!"

I feel my eyebrows shoot up. "Oh, I, uh…right then," I say eloquently. "I guess I'll—"

"Bye!" she shouts and closes the call.

I swallow and stare at the screen for a moment, my heart in my mouth. It takes me a few moments, but then I stir myself back to life and find Malyk's number.

It cuts off after a few rings, sending me to voice

mail. I'm not sure what to say, so I hang up, disappointed.

But a few seconds later, a text pops up, and my heart leaps back to life.

I can't talk now. I'm not sure what's going on. I'll text when I do. Love you, Mx

My hand is trembling as I read the message over and over. I'm still not clear what's happening, but the fact that he replied instantly and said that he loves me has my chest all filled with butterflies.

I might not know the details, but I can't help but cling to the hope that it's not over between me and Malyk. *Something's* in the works.

Now I just have to be patient and wait to see what it is.

I love you too, baby, I send back with a couple of hearts. Hope is raising me up again like a helium-filled balloon.

I tidy up my coffee table, then head to the fridge to crack open another beer. This one isn't a sad drink, though. It's a tentative celebration.

I look down at Samson, who's naturally followed me, his tail wagging as always. "Cheers," I say quietly to him, hoping that my optimism doesn't jinx anything.

By god, if things can go right for Malyk, if I can maybe find a way to keep him close to me, I don't think I'll ever stop celebrating for the rest of my life.

24

———

MALYK

I don't recognize the number on my phone. I take a breath before answering it. I really have no idea who it could be or if it'll be good or bad news. No doubt, knowing my luck, it'll be some recording asking if I've been in a car accident recently that wasn't my fault. Whatever happens, I brace myself and hit the answer button.

"Hello?" I say tentatively, then wince, wishing I'd sounded more confident.

"Ah, *there* you are, gorgeous. I didn't get a chance to speak to you before you ran away, and it took my people a while to get your number. Naughty boy."

I slowly stand up from where I was sitting on the end of my bed. "E-Emmalina?" I stammer.

"Yes, darling. You really shouldn't have snuck out like that. You worried me."

I swallow, guilt and shame prickling across my skin. "I'm so sorry. There was a bit of an incident and…" I break off what I was about to say. It's in the past now, and I don't want her to know. "I'm sorry. You're right. It was unbelievably rude of me to creep off without thanking you for your hospitality."

She tuts down the line. "Oh, I don't blame you, honey. You must have been upset. That awful agent of yours created quite the scene."

I hesitate a second, trying not to freak out. "You heard about that, did you?" I ask cautiously.

"I hear everything, doll," she replies in a tone that doesn't make me doubt that's true. "Anyway, I wanted to drop you a call and let you know that there's nothing to worry about anymore. That particular situation has all been fixed."

I blink and rub my chest. "It has?"

"Oh, yes," she says sounding rather smug. "He's *quite* fired, I think you'll find. A little birdie told me that he's been up to all sorts of horrible things. Mr. McKay decided that he wasn't a good fit for the agency's branding."

A laugh escapes my mouth before I can clap my hand over my face to stop it. But her repurposing Chris's exact words to me is too delicious.

"Oh, um, I'm glad to hear it," I say, trying to sound more professional and less like a cackling witch. "Does that mean that I'm not being let go?" I'm almost too afraid to ask, but I have to know. Chris could have done enough damage already.

"Well," she says, and I bite my lip in anticipation. "Of course you're not being let go, sweetie. That would be crazy. But obviously, you're going to have to switch to another agent now that Mr. Oakley is no longer with the company. From now on, you'll be represented by Jaye Broadhurst."

I frown and rack my brains. "Oh, I don't think I know him. Is he new?"

"No," she says casually. "He just works for the New York office."

My whole world tilts on its axis, and for a second, I forget how to breathe. "New York?" I eventually whisper.

"Yes," she says cheerfully. "I thought it made sense if you're going to be joining the Haus of Emmalina."

I drop back onto my bed with a thud, my hand flying back up to my mouth as tears fill my eyes. "What?" I squeak.

Her laugh is warm and kind. "Oh, silly me. Did I forget to mention that? That was another reason I was kind of mad you snuck out and left. I was going to tell you that you didn't need to leave at *all*. You're family now. Unless you'd rather stay in London? We do have a small contingency there, but—"

"No! No!" I blurt out before I can regain my composure. "I mean…what I mean is that relocating to New York would be a dream. An absolute dream. I'd be more than honored to join your company and switch to the McKay branch there. I don't know what to say other than thank you about a million times."

"Don't thank me, doll," she says devilishly. "Just get your ass over here. I'll have my people get in touch so we can book you flights and set you up in a room. I assume you'll need accommodation?"

It's an innocent-enough-sounding question, but I

get the implication. She's asking if I might have some-where else to live already.

That's a conversation for another time. I've got too much to think about right now, and I don't want to get overwhelmed. This is like winning the lottery, and I'm cautious about getting carried away and greedily wanting more.

"A room would be amazing," I say, managing to keep my voice from quivering. "And are you sure about the flight?"

She scoffs. "Of course, honey. We gotta get you in first class. Now you take care, and I'll see you real soon, all right?"

"Yes, thank you, bye," I manage to stammer before she hangs up.

I stare at the phone, not quite believing what just happened.

In fact, I know it won't seem real until I tell some-one, so I flick screens to my favorite contacts and hit the top one. "Mum?" I say, not really trusting my luck when she picks up after just a couple of rings.

"Malyk? Is everything okay?"

I don't blame her concern. My voice sounds ragged. I might not have told her all the ins and outs of getting my heart broken and losing my job all at once, but she's not an idiot.

"Uh…I think everything's amazing," I say with a nervous laugh. "I've been offered a permanent place with an incredible design house, and I'm switching agents." She knew about Chris and has never liked him, so that gets as big a gasp as the news about my new work.

"Sweetheart, that's incredible!" she cries out, already sounding tearful. "Is this because of the campaign you've been in for the make-up?"

"Sort of," I say. "But, Mum, there's a catch. I…it would mean moving to New York."

This gasp is the loudest of all. "New *York?*" she repeats. "Holy hollyhocks, that's amazing. Oh, hun. I'm so proud of you!"

I lick my lips. "You don't mind that I'd be moving away?"

Her sigh is patient and full of love. "I want you to follow your *dreams*. Besides, you already moved away a long time ago. So long as you still come home every once in a while and don't forget about your old mum, it'll be fine."

"I'd never forget about you," I say vehemently, making her laugh.

"Is this what you want?" she asks. "In your heart, is it telling you to go?"

I smile as salty tears run quietly into my mouth. "My heart is telling me to run to the airport as fast as I can."

"Well, there you go, then," she says. "What are you waiting for?"

I'm not so surprised by the flight this time. I can't believe this is my life now and I'm flying first class for the third time in so many weeks. But this time I only have a one-way ticket, and I spend the whole journey in nervous anticipation.

I've been deliberately vague with Oscar. Once I signed the contract with Emmalina and confirmed my move with McKay's to the New York office, I told him that I had good news and that I'd tell him everything soon. We've shared a few more messages since, and he keeps sending me photos of Samson, which I love.

But I've got half a plan to just show up at his apartment and surprise him. I'm going to see how I feel once I've dragged my three suitcases over to the house that I'm going to be sharing with some of Emmalina's other models. It looks a *lot* nicer than the place in London that I just quit, and I can't wait to get settled in.

After that, though, I'm getting in a cab and heading straight to Oscar's place. I keep trying to picture the look on his face when he opens his door. I'm just hoping beyond hope that now I'm going to be living in the same city as him he'll want to give our relationship a real chance.

I love him so much. But there's a part of me that's convinced that I can't be this lucky. That I can't possibly get my dream job *and* my dream man. That would be crazy.

Wouldn't it?

One of the other perks of flying in first is that we get to disembark the plane before anyone else, and also our luggage gets priority coming out on the belt. I have to wait for ages at passport control, but I can't explain the euphoria I feel when the guy at the booth asks me why I'm entering the country.

"I'm moving here for work," I tell him excitedly.

He cracks a small smile before handing me back my documents. "Welcome to the United States, sir," he says, then waves me through.

Despite all my luggage, I practically skip through into the departure hall. I don't really pay much attention to the people waiting around to greet loved ones or the drivers holding up names with signs. I'm busy looking for the directions to the subway, seeing as we didn't go that way last time.

But then my gaze is drawn to an enormous bouquet of red roses that make me smile. They're so beautiful, just seeing them brightens my day. Whoever they're for is lucky indeed.

Then the flowers shift, and all the breath leaves my body.

Because the person who's holding them is Oscar.

25

MALYK

I don't even think. I scream and let go of all my cases, breaking into a run. Oscar barely has time to move the bunch of roses aside before I launch myself at him, throwing my arms around his back and burying my face against his neck as I burst into tears.

"You're here! You're here!" I squeal over and over again. I'm vaguely aware of people around us going 'aww' and the sound of cameras clicking. I think it's nice, but I don't really care.

My whole being is consumed with the fact that the man I love is here and real and hugging me so tightly with the most romantic bouquet of flowers I've ever seen.

"I was going to surprise you," I complain weakly through my tears.

"Sorry, not sorry," he says with a chuckle. "Linny helped me beat you to it."

I draw back and wipe my face. "So you know?"

"That you've got a job here in the city and have

moved out indefinitely? Yeah, she thought I'd like to know."

"I wanted to make sure it was really, *really* real, then surprise you," I say guiltily.

But he grins and kisses my cheek so sweetly. "I know, baby. And I love that. But there was no *way* I wasn't going to meet you at the airport, and Emmalina knew that."

"I've got a room in a house," I tell him as I take another shaky breath, gradually recovering my composure. "I can give you the address."

But he shakes his head. "No, you don't have a room."

My stomach drops. "What? See? This is why I didn't want to tell you! I knew something was going to go wrong! I have to—"

He cups the side of my face with his free hand and cuts me off with a kiss. "You never had a room because I told Emmalina right away that you'd be moving in with me."

I blink for a few seconds. "You—I—what? Are you sure?"

"Baby," he says patiently. "I almost lost you once. I'm not losing you again. You'll live with me rent-free. And I'll also be sorting that credit card debt you thought you were hiding from me. This is a fresh start, and from now on, I'm not going to let anything stand in the way of me taking care of you."

My lip trembles, and I want to fight back. I want to protest that I can look after myself. But after almost losing *everything* this past week, I realize I don't have it in me anymore.

"Are you absolutely sure?" I check feebly.

"One hundred thousand percent," he says, drawing me into another hug, then handing me over my beautiful flowers.

"Oh, shit, my luggage," I say as I spin around in alarm. But there's someone standing next to it all, and they wave at me with a friendly smile.

Oscar and I approach the stranger with bright blue hair, several piercings and tattoos, and wearing a pair of tights that says they're ready for Hallowe'en all year round.

"Hi," they say with a little wave as we stop in front of them. "I kept watch over your stuff."

I let out a little whimper. I'm so tired and emotionally wrung out. "Thank you," I say sincerely.

They shift on their feet and fiddle with their phone in their hands. "I really hope you don't think I'm crazy," they say tentatively. "But I saw your friend with the roses and thought it might be an important reunion. I started filming when people began coming through the gate. I got the whole thing on camera."

My jaw drops open. "You did?" I cry. "Can we see?"

The person beams and turns their phone around, the video already queued up to play. I grip Oscar's hand tightly as we watch for a few seconds as the passengers in front of me come through the gate. And then there I am. When I see myself scream and run into Oscar's arms, I start crying again.

"That's beautiful," I manage to whisper. "Thank you. From the bottom of my heart."

"Would you like me to send it to you?" they offer.

"That would be amazing," I say.

It turns out their name is Zephyr, and I'm really glad to have their number now. I promise to text them as we part ways, and I wonder if I've just made my first friend here in New York.

Oscar helps me with all my luggage, and we make our way outside, where of course he has a private car waiting for us. I'm still shaking with adrenaline as we pull away from the curb, and for a while he just holds my hand and indulges me as I watch the video that Zephyr sent me over and over again.

Eventually, I resurface like I've come out of a trance and put my phone away, snuggling up against my man with a deep sigh. "I can't believe this is really happening."

He kisses forehead. "Part of me knows how insane the past few weeks have been," he admits. "But I absolutely believe this is happening because I wasn't going to have it any other way. As soon as I heard what Emmalina has orchestrated, it felt like everything fell into place."

He presses his lips to the back of my hand, and we share a warm smile. "Are you sure it's okay for me to move in?" I ask once more in a small voice. "It's super fast."

He tilts his head. "It's absolutely what I want. I'm so confident in us it seems crazy for you to live elsewhere and pay rent when you're just getting settled in a new city and starting out in a new job. But how do *you* feel?"

"Oh, I've already mentally unpacked," I say with a giddy laugh. "Besides, you can't uninvite me now. What would Samson say?"

He laughs and kisses my mouth sweetly. "I've been teasing him all day before I left for the airport," he confesses. "I kept saying 'Where's Malyk?' and then he'd bark his head off and start running around the apartment."

"You sod," I cry and poke his side. But I know he'd never, ever be mean to his dog, and I love the idea of Samson getting excited to see me again.

The journey into the city flies by. Between us, we manage to get all my bags out of the car along with the bouquet of roses, squish into the lift, then make it all the way to Oscar's apartment. Before we even open the door, I hear the barking and can't help but grin, thinking of when I first came here and met Samson. How much has happened since then.

Oscar takes my flowers and allows me to go in first and get mauled by an overexcited labradoodle. I laugh as Samson barks and whimpers as he headbutts me and jumps up to put his paws on my legs. I sit on the floor in the entrance hall and wrap my arms around him to give him a big hug and bury my face in his soft curls.

"Did you miss me, boy? I missed you, too."

Before I can finish my reunion and help, Oscar's already got everything inside the door and locked it up, shutting the rest of the world out. He places his keys into the bowl on the dresser, then picks something up and dangles it in front of me and Samson.

It's another key.

"For me?" I say stupidly. But for some reason, this is when it hits that he means it.

This is my home now.

He nods, and I pull myself up to my feet so I can take it but also wrap my arms around his waist and hug him tightly. "Thank you," I mumble. "Oscar…I'm so happy."

"Me too, baby. Come on, I've got a couple of things to show you."

We take off our shoes, and I groan after having mine on for so long, curling my toes in delight. He leads me to the kitchen, and I sit down at the breakfast bar. I wait as he pulls several things out of the fridge. "Linny sent a care package," he said. "Not everything got stored in the kitchen. Some things went straight to the bedroom," he says with a wiggle of his eyebrows.

I laugh and recall some of the kinkier items we only just got to start exploring while we were in Honeyrock. I hope Emmalina's given us even more fun items to try out.

For now, Oscar produces fresh strawberries and dipping chocolate that he heats in the microwave, along with little heart-shaped shortbread biscuits—or cookies, I guess I should call them. And of course, a bottle of Champagne and two of the saucers Emmalina was so fond of.

"She also sent a huge homemade lasagna to heat up

for later," Oscar explains as he pops the cork and pours the bubbly. "But I thought we'd start with this to toast."

"You know me—always hungry," I say, bouncing in my seat as he hands me my glass.

"I do know you," he says, his words overflowing with sincerity. He holds up his own glass, and I delicately tap mine to his. "To new beginnings," he says.

"To new love," I say, and it's so cheesy I want to cringe, but you know what? I don't, because it's true.

Before we sip, he leans over and kisses me gently. I've missed the way he tastes so much.

I nibble on a few strawberries, but I'm hungry for something else if I'm being honest. The last time we made love, it was so sad. I need to prove to myself that's all in the past now.

I think he senses my antsiness, and places his glass down before taking my hand. "Come on," he says as I do the same and stand up. "I've got something else to show you."

He leads me to his bedroom and opens the door. I gasp as I immediately see the clothes he's got hanging outside the doors of his wardrobe. There are a few layered on top of each other, but the first thing I notice is the teal blazer with the tropical bird print. The one I had to leave behind because we didn't have time to get it altered.

"Oscar...what?" I utter as I drift inside, looking at the garments. I recognize all of them.

"I had Briceson and his team keep working on everything you really loved but that didn't fit properly," he says, coming and hugging me from behind and kissing my neck. "For a while, I thought I'd ship them over to the UK, but then I realized they'd make a pretty awesome welcome home gift."

I turn in his arms and wrap mine around his neck, gazing into his hazel eyes. "You're the only welcome home gift I need," I say. Then after a pause… "But the clothes *are* absolutely lush as well. Thank you millions."

He grins and kisses me with a little more heat. *"Fuck,* I've missed you," he growls.

I waggle my eyebrows. "Do you want to show me how much?" I ask, pushing him toward the bed.

He doesn't answer with words. He drags my lower lip between his teeth, then spins us around and pushes me down onto the mattress, making me squeak and giggle. I scramble up backward, so my long legs are on the mattress, and watch as he crawls over me.

"What do you want, baby?" he asks as he kisses up my jaw and nibbles on my earlobe.

"Top me like this," I say, gripping his shoulders and wrapping my legs around his waist. "Kiss me and tell me you love me."

"All night," he promises, capturing my lips with his own.

Slowly, he peels my clothes off one item at a time. I had fully intended on showering all the airplane off me before doing anything intimate, but right now, I don't care. We're going to need a shower after this anyway, I'm sure. So why worry?

My hands work on undoing the buttons of his shirt and pushing it off his shoulders. Together, we get his jeans and underwear off, and then we're both gloriously naked again. It feels like this is the way it's always meant to be. My body and his, connected as one.

For a while, we simply rut together with him on top of me, our cocks sliding against each other, trapped between us. But then he gets out a bottle of lube, and I realize it's the last one from the three-pack Emmalina gave us that we never got to use. It's Sex on the Beach flavor, and I'm glad we waited until now to break this one out.

This is definitely a party.

He stretches me out, but I'm impatient. "I'm ready," I say, even when I could probably do with a few more minutes. But I can stretch myself around his cock. I just need him inside me *now*.

He laughs at me but kisses my neck with a hum as well. "All right, baby brat."

"Show me what you got, old man," I tease with a devilish grin.

He suits up and coats himself with lube, but then he's forcing his way inside me, and I'm groaning and whimpering. I won't admit that it's a bit much too fast, but I think he knows, as he goes slowly as he gradually fills me up.

I cling to him and rub our temples together. "Oscar —oh," I utter.

This is *my* bed now, with *my* man. For the first time since we met, there's no ticking clock looming over us. We're free.

When I'm ready, he starts moving within me leisurely, pulsing against my prostate and lighting me up from inside. I'm his, and he's mine, and nothing is going to tear us apart again.

He brings me to the point of bliss, and we come together. I've never felt so safe or so cherished.

He was right with his toast. This is a new beginning for both of us. It's the start of our new life together.

And I can't wait to see where that journey takes us.

EPILOGUE
OSCAR

One Year Later

It's official. My favorite accessory of this year's spring/summer collection is the smile Malyk wears as he stomps down this Paris runway.

It's quite subtle because he's supposed to keep it neutral, but I always spot it just as he's about to turn around. The way his lips quirk a fraction and his eyes flick up and down the audience like he knows they're eating him up.

Emmalina asked me to work this show, but I declined. I'll do the next one. This time, I just want to give my baby every second of my attention during his sensational Paris Fashion Week debut.

He's done New York and London already, but Emmalina wanted to make sure he was seasoned before he came to France. That way, he'd capture everyone's attention in all the right ways. She wasn't wrong. His confidence is natural and inviting, drawing the audience in like he's whispering a secret to them. I'm so incredibly proud to witness his debut in all its glory.

Everything's been better since Malyk came into my life. Or rather—since he came *back* into my life. He fills my home with joy and vitality. Thanks to his infectious passion, I've been able to reconnect with my love of fashion photography again. I'd been on the verge of quitting altogether, but when I suddenly had him as my muse twenty-four seven, it was so much easier to find my inspiration once more.

But also…I just take photos for fun as well, without the pressure of what's going to sell. Urban landscapes, nature, wildlife—anything I think is beautiful. Malyk encouraged me to set up an Instagram account of my own, and I was amazed that people wanted to follow it.

He wasn't. After Samson, he's my biggest fan.

The feeling is mutual.

It's been such a privilege watching him blossom in New York. We've visited London a couple of times for work, and went to Newport for Christmas to spend the holiday in Wales with his mum, but I truly believe New York is the city he belongs in.

Which is a relief because I'm not letting him go anywhere if I can help it.

It took him a while to fully settle into the apartment. For a long time, he kept thinking of himself as a guest still. His attitude seemed to really change, though, when I surprised him one day by hanging a couple of large canvas prints in our bedroom.

The first was one of the selfies we took before the

ball. I know that evening ended badly, but those photos were so full of our blossoming love, and they were the first we took together as a couple. I just had to hang one up to remind us of that. The second was one of the artful nudes I took of him on the bed covered in rose petals. He looks so breathtaking in that one, and I think looking at that regularly helped him to see himself through my eyes.

After that, I noticed a lot more of his stuff spreading out, and it made me ridiculously happy to know that he's here to stay.

I don't think Emmalina or Jaye, his new agent, would allow him to leave either, to be fair. Since he got out from under Oakley's manipulative grasp, he's been inundated with work. And why wouldn't he be? He's the star of every room he walks into, always pulling focus, no matter who else is there.

I love that he's not forgotten who he is, though. He calls his mum every week, and despite making loads of new friends, he still keeps in touch with Jamie back in London and Frans in Stockholm (who thankfully never dated Oakley). Both of them are thriving with their own agents and careers now, and the three young men have agreed to meet up here in Paris while fashion week is going on. I love seeing my baby's friendships grow internationally.

He hangs out with Zephyr back home regularly, but they always do down-to-earth things like shopping in thrift stores. He takes out the garbage when it's his turn and walks Samson in the rain without complaint. He might look like some sort of goddess, but he's still a mere mortal like the rest of us, and I feel blessed that he's chosen me to walk this life with.

For a while, I worried about our age difference. That he hadn't had enough dating experience to really want to settle down. But the one time I was finally brave enough to bring it up, he scoffed and asked if he'd already won the jackpot, why would he need to still fuck around for pennies on the slot machines?

Thanks to that impassioned speech, we spent a filthy long weekend in Vegas to fuck around on some actual slot machines, but the real jackpot was back in the bedroom, as it always is with him.

God, I thought I was slowing down as I approached my mid-forties. But it turns out that with the right partner, I'm still quite the monster in the sack. It helps that my baby is always hungry—for food and other delights.

The show is coming to an end, and the models all are parading down the catwalk one last time. I cheer and clap from my seat as Emmalina takes her turn in a sublime evening dress that looks like raindrops glistening on a rose. She bows for her applause on another wonderful collection, then graciously accepts an enormous colorful bouquet of mixed flowers and a magnum of Champagne.

I'm sure that will be put to good use at the afterparty, but Malyk and I will have to hear about it later. I'm taking him for dinner inside the Eiffel Tower to celebrate his Paris debut. That's on the second floor. But first, we're going right to the top to the Champagne bar to have some bubbly of our own.

Little does he know that the whole place will be just for us.

With a little help from my good friend who adores some drama, there's going to be a carpet of rose petals leading to a small table set for two where a ridiculously expensive bottle will be chilling with two glasses. There's going to be a string quartet who'll know to start playing when I text the events manager from the bottom of the tower. I've been making a list of Malyk's favorite sappy tracks from his streaming collection, and the musicians have learned them all. The only thing that could make it more perfect would be having Samson there with us. But if all goes well, I hope that he'll be our ring bearer on a very special day in the near future.

I thought I'd be more nervous as I greet him afterward and our night together begins. I guess I'm a little anxious about the logistics. But I'm mostly just incredibly excited to see the look on his face when I pop the question.

I behave myself. I don't touch my jacket pocket once we leave the show and walk to our taxi. I know the ring—emeralds set into a platinum band—green and silver just like his eyes—is securely buttoned in and not going anywhere. I do play with his fingers as we make our way through the traffic, though.

"You were magnificent," I murmur.

He beams at me. The smile on the runway might have been subtle, but this one could light up the whole city. "You already said that," he teases. "Just once or twice."

I don't care. I just kiss his cheek and inhale the scent

that's so uniquely him, even with the sweet perfume he's wearing that smells like candy. "Only once or twice? Damn. I'll have to try harder."

He laughs freely and beautifully, and it's all I can do to keep my hands off him for the rest of the drive there.

I glance surreptitiously at him several times as we make our way over to the desk where they'll arrange for our transportation up in the elevator. He's wearing the stunning teal blazer that Briceson tailored for him back in New York, strutting like a peacock and making heads turn as always.

He doesn't seem to suspect a thing.

"This is stunning," he says in awe as he looks up at the monument looming above us. I take the opportunity to quickly text the events manager, then rub his back. "I'm not sure what's best," I admit. "Being able to see it from so many places in the city or the view from the top."

"You're the best view," he says playfully with a kiss.

Okay…now I might have a few flutterings of nerves. I just want this to be perfect because he's perfect. I take a breath before entering the elevator at the bottom of the tower, rehearsing what I want to say.

I've taken a risk and also arranged for the whole thing to be filmed. Just on a regular phone—they're such damned good quality these days—but I've hired a professional videographer to make sure it's in focus and all that jazz. With my permission, Malyk posted our reunion video on his Instagram, and it got millions of views. It was insane.

Usually, I shy away from being on that side of the

lens, but this is both my and Malyk's journey now. I think he'd love the idea of showing the sequel to the world.

And if not, then it can just be a keepsake for the two of us. Win-win. But as a photographer, I do appreciate capturing the moment for prosperity either way.

Despite all my cool bravado, my heart is hammering as the elevator reaches the top floor. I take another slow deep breath. Malyk maybe notices something that time and squeezes my hand. "Don't worry. It's not *that* high," he says. Bless him. I'm not great with tall buildings—as we found out at the top of the Shard in London—but the fact that he remembered that and thought I'd brought him here despite my fear anyway is very sweet.

No, I tested out the height yesterday while he was working. I'm nervous for an entirely different reason now.

As soon as the doors open, the sound of the quartet fills the air. Thankfully, it's not a particularly windy day, so the notes travel beautifully over the night air. We step out directly onto the walkway, and as promised, it's covered in rose petals. The musicians and the videographer are to the left, and our little table is at the end on the right with the bucket of Champagne, and everything is perfect.

I look to Malyk, who's gone very still.

He turns to me as the elevator doors close, and his eyes go wide.

It's now or never.

I take both his hands and squeeze them in mine.

Then I lower to one knee.

He screams and drops my hands to cover his mouth. If it's possible, his eyes have gone even bigger, and he starts shaking his head.

"No, no, no!" he shrieks, but it's definitely a happy sort of surprise, so I don't hesitate. Calmly, I reach inside my jacket, unbutton the pocket, and retrieve the ring box.

I'm completely thrown when Malyk runs several feet away, gripping his hair, his mouth hanging open.

"No!" he yells again with a laugh. "No, you're kidding me? No!"

I start to worry.

But I don't say anything as he comes back to me, trembling like he's freezing, even though the air is quite balmy. Then I understand why.

Because he also drops to one knee in front of me and pulls a different ring box out of his beautiful teal jacket.

I feel my own jaw go slack as I stare at it, and he starts laughing hard. His whole body is vibrating. But then he shakes himself and blinks.

"Let's open them together on three," he suggests.

I'm too stunned to do anything but nod. He counts, and then we're both revealing our rings at the same time.

The one he's got me has amber stones set in rose gold.

Like hazel to match my eyes.

He makes an adorable sound as he takes in what I've bought for him, then our gazes meet. His eyes are wet like mine.

"On three?" I suggest.

He nods and counts softly.

"Will you marry me?" we say at the same time.

He bursts into tears and throws his arms around me. I hold him like it's the only thing keeping me anchored to this great monument.

"You almost out-surprised me again," he says thickly.

"No," I say, my voice also catching. "You *definitely* out-surprised me."

He leans back and carefully wipes his eyes so as not to smudge his make-up, then he grins. "Answers on three or right now?"

"Right now," I say, my whole body trembling. I raise my eyebrows, open my mouth and—

"*Yes!*" we both cry.

There's more laughing, more tears, and eventually, we manage to get our rings on each other's fingers.

They look incredible.

I point out the camera to Malyk, and he gasps in happiness and delight. Proudly, we show off our new bling, and then the recording ends.

So that's what the world will watch—and believe me, that one goes *truly* viral.

What viewers at home don't see is the way Malyk cries in my arms afterward and tells me he loves me about a hundred times. They don't see me lose my shit either, and that's a good thing because I'm a *far* less pretty crier than he is. They don't see us drinking the very expensive Champagne far too quickly to truly appreciate it. They don't see us slow dancing to one song, then singing along terribly to the next.

Because some memories are so precious, they don't need to be recorded on film. Those moments will live freshly in our minds for the rest of our lives. And the most important thing is for us to be present and alive for nothing but each other.

This night I make a promise to do that for all time, and so does Malyk.

My beautiful muse. My adorable brat. My baby. I'm going to spend the rest of our lives capturing him on camera for the world to see but also just because I can for myself. He's the center of my world. My inspiration. My one and only.

Forever.

Thank you so much for reading Malyk and Oscar's story! If you enjoyed it, please leave a review so that others can discover it as well.

Make sure you don't miss all the other Model Love books! They can all be read as stand alones, but with so many happily ever afters to discover, why not try them all?

Check out the full series here or see the full list of titles on the next page.

Scout. But Emery's life is in danger thanks to his out and proud charity work, and once he finally recognizes Scout, their chemistry in undeniable.

-

Homeward Bound

Swift Coal just found out he's a father, and his daughter (and her cranky cat) are coming to stay. His best friend's younger brother, Micha Perkins, has nowhere to go and a wrongfully tattered reputation. He's relieved when Swift asks him to be a live-in babysitter. He just has to hide his lifelong crush. Easy, because Swift is straight—right?

-

Bright Horizon

With sixteen years between them, baker Ben Turner and lawyer Elias Solomon have no idea their crush is mutual. But when Ben inherits his long-lost family's estate and becomes an overnight millionaire, Elias swears to protect the innocent younger man from the vultures circling him. To unravel the mystery of the inheritance, they must go to England to confront Ben's estranged relatives…and their feelings for each other.

-

Crossed Paths

Raj Bhat is done living in the shadows. It's time for him to take charge of his own destiny and tell the man he's fallen for how he really feels.

-

Midnight Sky

It's the night before New Year's Eve. Taylan Demir is all

alone, and he's just lost his dog. Except when his handsome customer, Hudson Perkins, comes to his rescue, Taylan doesn't just get his dog back. He's suddenly got a hot date, and maybe someone to kiss when the clock strikes midnight.

-

Memory Lane

Angel Shields saved Jay Coal's life in high school, and Jay has secretly loved his straight best friend ever since. Now Angel's back in town with amnesia after a suspicious work accident and it's Jay's turn to rescue him. He pretends to be Angel's fiancé to see him in the hospital, but with his scrambled-up memory, Angel's not sure it's fictional after all. He just knows he loves Jay more than ever.

-

Thin Ice

Kamran's ex broke his heart, tricked him into aiding a bank robbery, and now he wants him to do one last job. There's only one way to say no: seek the protective custody of the biggest, grumpiest FBI agent ever, Lee Marshall. And pretend to be his boyfriend for a week-long family reunion in their giant mansion. Wait, what?

-

Calm Shores

Gorgeous, sophisticated Dante walks into Oliver's bar and orders…a boyfriend?! Dante needs a man to keep his mother from setting him back up with his awful, cheating ex, and Oliver is up for the challenge.

-

Fresh Snow

Emery Klein is throwing the best Christmas party ever, but his fiancé, Scout Duffy, and all their friends have something more exciting in mind.

-

Each Pine Cove book can be read as a stand alone and has its own happy ever after. But if you read the whole series, you'll see a lot of familiar faces!

Click here to get the Pine Cove eBook bundle

Click here to get the Pine Cove audio bundle

ABOUT THE AUTHOR

HJ Welch is an author of contemporary MM romance series, including the international bestselling Pine Cove series. She lives just outside of London with her husband and two balls of fluff that occasionally pretend to be cats. She began writing at an early age, later honing her craft online in the world of fanfiction on sites like Wattpad. Fifteen years and over half a million words later, she sought out original MM novels to read. By the end of 2016 she had written her first book of her own, and in 2017 she achieved her lifelong dream of becoming a full-time author. When she's not writing she's usually dancing, singing, filming music videos, taking long walks, working on jigsaw puzzles, drinking prosecco, or talking about Eurovision.

She also writes contemporary British MM fairy tale adaptations as Helen Juliet.

You can contact Helen via the following:

Newsletter: https://www.subscribepage.com/helenjuliet

Website – www.hjwelch.com

Facebook Group – Helen's Jewels
Instagram – @helenjwrites
Twitter – @helenjwrites
Book Bub – @HJWelchAuthor
Facebook Page – @HJWelchAuthor

9 781739 339012